THE VANISHINGS

The Vanishings

LEFT BEHIND™

>THE KIDS<

Jerry B. Jenkins

Tim LaHaye

TYNDALE
KIDS

TYNDALE HOUSE PUBLISHERS, INC.
WHEATON, ILLINOIS

To our own kids

Contents

1

THE FOUR KIDS

ONE

Judd—
The Runaway

JUDD Thompson Jr. had always hated having the same name as his father. Until now.

Every time the phone rang and someone asked for Judd, it was "Which one? Big Judd or Little Judd?" The funny thing was, Little Judd was already taller than his father. He had just gotten his driver's license, and the whiskers on his chin formed a thin goatee. He was tired of being called *Junior*, and if he were never called Little Judd again for the rest of his life, it would be too soon.

But now, for once, being Judd Thompson Jr. was working in Judd's favor.

This break was meant to be, Judd decided. After days of fighting with his parents about where he was going, who he was with, what he was doing, and how late he would be in, he had just happened to be home one afternoon. And his mother picked that day to ask him to bring in the mail. If that didn't prove this was meant to be, Judd didn't know what did.

Judd sighed loudly at his mother's request. She said he acted like any small chore or favor was the biggest burden in the world. That was exactly how he felt. He didn't want to be told to do anything.

"Why can't *you* get it?" he asked her.

"Because I asked you to," she said.

"Why do *I* have to do everything?"

"Would you like to compare what you do around here with what I do?" she asked, and that began the usual argument. Only when his mother threatened to ground him did he stomp out to the mailbox. He was glad he did.

On the way back to the house, idly flipping through catalogs and letters and magazines, he had found it—an envelope addressed to him. It was clearly a mistake—obviously intended for his father. He knew that as soon as he saw it. It was business mail. He didn't recognize the return address.

Just to be ornery, he slipped it inside his jacket and gave the rest of the mail to his mother. Well, he didn't actually give it to her. He tossed it onto the kitchen table in front of her, and half of it slid to the floor. He headed to his room.

"Just a minute, young man," she said, using another of his least favorite names. "Get back here and give me this mail properly."

"In a minute," he said, jogging up the steps.

"Oh, never mind," she said. "By the time you get back here, I'll have it picked up, read, and answered."

"You're welcome!" he hollered.

"A job not finished is not worthy of a thank-you," she said. "But thanks anyway."

Judd took off his jacket, cranked up his music, and lay on his bed, opening the envelope. Onto his chest dropped a credit card in his name, Judd Thompson Jr. A sticker on it told him to call a toll-free number and answer a few questions so he could begin using the card. The letter told him they had honored his request. He could spend tens of thousands of dollars using that card alone.

Judd couldn't believe his luck. He dialed the number and was asked his mother's maiden name and his date of birth. He knew enough to use his grandmother's maiden name and his father's birthday. This was, after all, really his father's card, wrong name or not. The automated voice told Judd he could begin using the card immediately.

It was then that he planned his escape.

Judd felt desperate to get away. He wasn't sure what had happened or why, but he was sure his family was the problem.

Judd's father owned a business in Chicago and was wealthy. His mother had never had to work outside the home. Judd's little brother and sister, nine-year-old twins Marc and Marcie, were young enough to stay out of his hair. They were OK, he guessed.

Marc's and Marcie's rooms were full of trophies from church, the same as Judd's had once been. He had really been into that stuff, memorizing Bible verses, going to camp every summer, all that.

But when Judd had gone from the junior high to the senior high youth group at New Hope Village Church in Mount Prospect, Illinois, he seemed to lose interest overnight. He used to invite his friends to church and youth group. Now he was embarrassed to say his parents made him go.

Judd felt he had outgrown church. It had been OK when he was a kid, but now nobody wanted to dress like he did, listen to his kind of music, or have a little fun. At school he hung with kids who got to make their own decisions and do what they wanted to do. That was all he wanted. A little freedom.

Even though they could afford it, Judd's parents refused to buy him his own car. How many other high school juniors still rode the bus to school? When Judd did get to drive one of his parents' cars, one of them told him where he could go, whom he could go with, what he could do, and when he had to be back.

If only his parents knew what he was doing when they thought he was "just out with the guys," Judd thought. How he hated his curfew, his parents' constant watch over his schoolwork, their criticizing his hair, his clothes, and his friends.

Worst of all, he was grounded if he didn't get up for Sunday school and church every Sunday. Just the Sunday before, he had put up such a fuss that his mother had come into his room and sat on his bed. "Don't you love Jesus anymore?" she asked.

What a stupid question, Judd thought. He didn't remember ever really loving Jesus. Oh, he had liked all the stories and knew a lot of verses. But loving Jesus? Loving God? That was for little kids and old ladies. But what could he say to his mother?

"If you want the truth, I only go to church so I can go out on weekends and use the car."

That was clearly not what she had wanted

to hear. "All right then, just forget it!" she said.

"I can stay home from church?"

"If you don't want to go anywhere for a week."

Judd swore under his breath. It was a good thing his mother hadn't heard *that*. He'd have been grounded for life.

In Sunday school, Judd copped an attitude. He wore clothes his parents only barely approved of, and he stayed as far away as possible from the "good" kids. What losers! They never had any fun. Judd didn't smile, didn't carry a Bible, didn't look at the teacher, didn't say anything. When the teacher asked his opinion of something, he shrugged. He wanted everyone to know he was there only because he had to be.

In church, he slouched when his father wasn't looking. He wanted to burrow within himself and just make it through to the end of the service. He didn't sing along, he didn't bow his head during prayer, he didn't shut his eyes. No one had ever said those were rules; Judd was simply trying to be different from everyone else. He was way too cool for this stuff.

As usual, Pastor Vernon Billings got off on his kick about what he called the Rapture. "Someday," he said, "Jesus will return to take his followers to heaven. Those who have received him will disappear in the time it takes to blink your eye. We will disappear right in front of disbelieving people. Won't that be a great day for us and a horrifying one for them?"

The kindly old pastor talked about how important it was for everyone to be sure of his own standing before God and to think and pray about friends and loved ones who might not be ready. Judd's little secret was that he had never really believed any of that.

He'd had enough chances. At vacation Bible school, his friends had prayed and received Christ. He was embarrassed. He told them he had already done that at home. At camp a few years later, Judd felt guilty and sinful when a young speaker talked about church kids who weren't really Christian believers. He had wanted to go forward; he really had. But he had also just been named Camper of the Week for memorizing a bunch of Bible verses and being the fastest to look up some others. What would people say?

Judd knew he didn't have to go forward or talk with anyone to receive Christ. He knew he could do it by himself. He could pray sincerely and ask God to forgive his sins and make Jesus the Lord of his life. But later, when the meeting was over and the emotion wore off, he told himself that was something he could do anytime.

Judd felt the most guilty when he was twelve years old and many of his Sunday school classmates signed up to be baptized. Their teacher and Pastor Billings made clear to them that this was an act of obeying Christ, a step taken by Christians to declare themselves followers of Jesus.

As the students were baptized, they were asked to tell about when they had received Christ. Judd had done the unthinkable. He had quoted Scripture and made up a story about when he had become a Christian "once by myself at camp."

He felt guilty about that for weeks, never having the guts to tell his parents or his Sunday school teacher. Yet something kept him from confessing to God and getting things right with Christ. Now he was sixteen and had feelings and thoughts he believed no one would understand. He was bored with his church, frustrated with his parents, and secretly proud that he wasn't really part of the church crowd. He went because he had to, but someday soon he would make his own decisions.

With the small error on that credit card, Judd Thompson Jr. had his ticket to freedom. He had seen his dad get cash with his credit card at the bank and at the automatic teller machines. And he knew that almost anything could be paid for with that magic card.

Of course, one day the bill would come and his parents would be able to trace where he had been. But he could put a lot of miles between himself and them in the meantime.

For several days, Judd saved cash, withdrawing as much as he could each day from the automatic teller machine. He hid the money with the passport he had gotten the year before when his father took him along on a business trip to Asia. He had been miserable on that trip and let his dad know it every chance he got. Judd Sr. had finally given up trying to convince Judd Jr. that this was "the opportunity of a lifetime."

Secretly Judd had to admit that he enjoyed the hotels, the meals, and even learning how to get around in foreign cities with different cultures and languages. But he wasn't about to tell his dad that. Judd knew Dad had dragged him along only to get him away from his new friends, the ones his mother called the "evil influences." It was also supposed to be a time for him and his dad to bond—whatever that meant. Dad had tried, Judd had to give him that, but there had been no bonding. Mostly it was just Judd

11

scowling, complaining, arguing, and begging to go home.

At least he got a passport out of the deal. That, along with his new driver's license and the credit card, gave him what he thought was complete freedom. A friend had told him he looked old enough to pass for twenty-one and that he should get a fake identification card that would allow him to buy liquor in Illinois. It was cheaper and easier than he thought to get both his driver's license and his passport copied with a new birth date.

His plan was to take his stash of cash and go to O'Hare International Airport some night. He would take the first flight he could get to another English-speaking country. Beyond that, his plan was not clear. One thing was sure: He wasn't going to bum around begging for a place to stay. He would live first-class all the way.

Now Judd was a criminal. He told himself he wasn't scared. Breaking the law only made him bolder about his plan, and he began making up reasons why he had to get away from home as soon as possible.

As he made his plans, Judd became more and more angry. He disagreed with everything his parents did or said. He was mean and sarcastic.

One day after school his little brother came into his room.

"What do *you* want?" Judd asked Marc.

"I just wanted to ask you a question. Are you still a Christian?"

Judd lied. "Of course," he said. "What's it to you?"

"I was just wonderin' because it doesn't seem like you're happy or acting like one."

"Why don't you get out of here and mind your own business!"

"Will you be mad at me if I pray for you?"

"Don't waste your breath."

"You're makin' Mom cry, you know that?"

"She shouldn't waste her tears either."

"Judd, what's the matter? You used to care—"

"Out! Get out!"

Marc looked pale and tearful as he left. Judd shook his head, disgusted, and told himself Marc would be a lot better off when he outgrew his stupidity. *I used to be just like that,* Judd thought. *What a wuss!*

Judd stuffed some of his favorite clothes in his book bag and jogged downstairs. "And where do you think you're going, mister?" his mother said. Did she always have to talk like that? Couldn't she just ask a simple question?

"I'm going to the library to study," Judd

said. "I'll be there till closing, so don't wait up for me."

"Since when did you get interested in studying?" his mother asked.

"You said you wanted my grades to improve!"

"You don't need to go to the library to study, Judd. Why don't you stay here and—"

"I need some peace and quiet, all right?"

"What will you do for dinner?"

"I'll get something out."

"Do you need some money?"

"No! Now leave me alone!"

"All right! Just go! But don't be late!"

"Mom! I already told you! I'm staying till closing, so—"

"Don't wait up, yeah, I know. Are you meeting someone there?"

"No!"

"I'd better not find out you've been out with your friends, young man. . . ."

But Judd was already out the door.

* * *

At O'Hare, Judd found a flight on Pan-Continental Airlines that left early in the evening and was scheduled to arrive in London the following morning. His phony identification cards worked perfectly, and he enjoyed being referred to as Mr. Thompson. His first-class ticket was very expensive, but it was the only seat left on the 747.

Judd knew it wouldn't be long before his parents started looking for him. They would discover his car at the airport, and they would quickly find his name on the passenger list of the Pan-Con flight. He'd better enjoy this freedom while he could, he decided. He would try to hide in England for as long as possible, but even if he was found and hauled back to the United States, he hoped he would have made his point.

What was his point, exactly, he wondered. That he needed his freedom. Yeah, that was it. He needed to be able to make some decisions on his own, to be treated like an adult. He didn't want to be told what to do all the time. He wanted the Thompson family to know that he was able to get along in the world on his own. Going to London by himself, based on his own plans, ought to prove that.

Judd sat on the aisle. On the other side of the aisle sat a middle-aged man who had three drinks set before him. Beyond him, in the window seat, a younger man sat hunched over his laptop computer.

Judd was stunned at the beauty of the flight attendant, whose name badge read

"Hattie." He'd never known anyone with that name, but he couldn't work up the courage to say so. He was excited and pleased with himself when she didn't even ask to see any identification when she offered him champagne.

"How much?" he asked.

"It's free in first class, Mr. Thompson," she said.

He had tried champagne a few times and didn't like it, but he liked the idea of its sitting on the tray table in front of him. He would pretend to be on business, on his way to London for important meetings.

Captain Rayford Steele came over the intercom, announcing their flight path and altitude and saying he expected to arrive at Heathrow Airport at six in the morning.

Judd Thompson Jr. couldn't wait. This was already the most exciting night of his life.

TWO

Vicki—
The Rebel

VICKI Byrne was fourteen and looked eighteen. Tall and slender, she had fiery red hair and had recently learned to dress in a way that drew attention, from girls and guys. She liked leather. Low cut black boots, short skirts, flashy tops, lots of jewelry, and a different hairstyle almost every day.

She was tough. She had to be. Other kids at school considered kids who lived in trailer parks lower class. Vicki's friends were her "own kind," as her enemies liked to say. When she and her trailer park neighbors boarded the bus on Vicki's first day of high school, they quickly realized how it was going to be.

The bus was full. It was obvious the trailer park was the last stop on the route. Only the first two kids of the twelve boarding from the trailer park found a seat even to share. Every morning they jostled for position to be one of the lucky first ones aboard. Vicki had given up trying. Two senior boys, smelling of tobacco and bad breath and never, ever, carrying schoolbooks, muscled their way to the front of the line.

No one on the bus looked at the trailer park kids. They seemed to be afraid that if they made eye contact, they might have to slide over and make room for a third person in their seat. And, of course, no one wanted to sit next to "trailer trash." Vicki had seen them hold their noses when she and her neighbors boarded, and she had heard the whispers.

How was a freshman girl supposed to feel when people pretended not to see her, pretended she didn't exist, acted as if she were scum?

The bus driver refused to pull away from the trailer park until everyone was seated, so the two senior trailer boys—who had already found seats—rose and scowled and insisted that people make room. Some "rich kids," which they all seemed to be if they didn't live near Vicki, begrudgingly made room.

The first day, Vicki had found herself the last to find a seat. She looked in the front, where most of the black kids sat. They had to be among the first on the bus, because no one seemed to want to sit with them either—especially the trailer park kids. In fact, Vicki's friends called the black kids horrible names and wouldn't sit with them even if they offered a seat.

Vicki had been raised to believe black kids were beneath her too. No black people lived in the trailer park, and she didn't know why they were supposed to be inferior, other than that they were a different color. Her father had said they were lazy, criminal, stupid. And yet that was how Vicki saw her father himself. At least until two years before.

When she was twelve, something had happened to her parents. Before that they had seemed the same as most of their neighbors. Every Friday night there was a community dance where drunk and jealous husbands fought over their wives and girlfriends. It was not unusual for the dances to be broken up by the police, with one or more of the fighters being hauled off to jail for the night. Often, her mother bailed out Vicki's dad, and then they would fight over that for the rest of the weekend.

Vicki's father had trouble keeping a job, and her mother's waitressing didn't pay enough to cover their bills. Vicki's dad had been a mechanic, a construction worker, a short-order cook, and a cashier at a convenience store. Being arrested or late or absent from work one too many times always cost him his job, and then they would live on welfare for a few months until he could find something else.

Vicki had wished her parents would stay away from the community dance every Friday night, but they seemed to look forward to it as the highlight of their week. She had to admit she used to love hanging around with her older brother Eddie and little sister Jeanni and their friends during those dances. They were always off sneaking around and getting into mischief while their parents danced, sang, drank, and fought. It was while running with those kids that Vicki learned to smoke and drink. When Eddie graduated from high school, he moved out on his own to Michigan.

There were a few trailer park families who never came to the dances. They, Vicki's father said, were the "religious types. The goody-goodies. The churchgoers."

Vicki's mother often reminded him, "Don't forget, Tom, that was the way I was raised. And it's not all bad. We could do with some church around here."

"I rescued you from all that superstitious mumbo jumbo," he had said.

That became Vicki's view of church. She believed there was a God out there some-where, and her mother told her he had cre-ated the world and created her and loved her. She couldn't make that make sense. If God created this lousy world and her lousy life, how could he love her?

One Friday night when Vicki was in sev-enth grade, the family heard the loud music signaling the weekly dance and began moseying to the parking lot to hear the band. Vicki's plan was to ditch Jeanni as soon as the party started and run off somewhere with her friends to sneak some cigarettes and maybe some beer.

But before she could do that, the music stopped and everyone looked toward the small stage in surprise. "Uh, 'scuse me," the lead singer said. "One of our neighbors here has asked if he can introduce a guest who'd like to speak to us for a few minutes."

Sometimes local politicians said a few words at the dances, or the police reminded people to behave, or the landlord reminded everyone that "this is a privilege and can be ended if there are more fights."

But the neighbor with a guest speaker had never been seen at one of these dances. He was one of those church people Vicki's dad made fun of. And his guest was a preacher.

As soon as he began to speak, people groaned and began shouting to "get on with the music."

But the speaker said, "If you'll just indulge me for a few moments, I promise not to take more than five minutes of your time. And I plead with you to let your children hear this too."

Somehow, that quieted the crowd. The man launched into a very fast, very brief message that included verses from the Bible and a good bit of shouting. Vicki had been to church only once with a friend, and she had no idea what he was talking about. She was struck, however, that everyone, even the bartenders and musicians, seemed to stop and listen. No one ran around, no one spoke, no one moved.

The speaking didn't seem all that great, but there was a feeling, an atmosphere. The man seemed to know what he was talking about and spoke with confidence and authority. The best Vicki could figure out, he was saying that everyone was a sinner and needed God. God loved them and wanted to forgive their sins and promise to take them to heaven when they died.

She didn't believe him. She hated her life, and if she did things wrong, they weren't any worse than what her own parents did. They smoked and drank and fought. What was the big deal? And if God loved them, why were they living in a trailer park?

Vicki wanted to get going, to run with her friends, but she didn't want to be the only one moving. Everyone else seemed frozen in place. Vicki didn't understand it. She hadn't heard too much of this religious talk, and she didn't care to hear any more. When she turned to complain to her parents, she was shocked to see her mother standing there with her eyes closed, silently moving her lips. Could she be praying?

And her father! Usually something like this would make him nervous and fidgety. It wouldn't have surprised her if he had tried to shout down the speaker or cause some other disturbance. But there he stood, staring at the preacher, not moving. "Daddy?" she whispered.

He held up a hand to shush her. What was so interesting? What was keeping all these party people quiet? The preacher asked his listeners to bow their heads and close their eyes. Now *there* was something they would never do. If there was anything Vicki's dad and his friends hated more than being told what to do, she didn't know what it was.

When she looked around, however, almost everyone was doing it! Some just stared at the ground, but most had their eyes closed. The preacher told them how they could receive Christ. "Tell God you realize you're a sinner," he said. "Thank him for sending Jesus to die for you, and accept his offer of forgiveness."

Vicki still didn't understand. The whole thing made her uneasy, but something was happening here. She looked to her dad and was stunned to see he had fallen to his knees and was crying. Her mother crouched next to him, hugging him and praying with him.

Vicki was embarrassed. As soon as the preacher finished and the music started again, she slipped away with her friends. "What was that all about?" she asked them.

"Who knows?" a boy said, pulling cans of beer from a paper bag and passing them around. "You ought to ask your old man. He really seemed into it. Your mom too."

Vicki shrugged. Her girlfriend added, "They left the dance, you know."

"What do you mean?" Vicki asked.

"Your mom was leading your dad back to the trailer, and your little sister was tagging along behind them. They must've got religion or something."

"Whatever that means," Vicki said, hoping to change the subject. "I need a cigarette."

Vicki didn't really need a cigarette. It was

just something to say that made her feel older. She smoked, yes, but she didn't carry a pack with her. She just bummed smokes off her friends once in a while.

At the end of the evening, when she and her friends had had enough beer and cigarettes to make her feel wasted, she filled her mouth with gum to try to hide the smell and made her way back home. She walked through the parking lot where the music and the dancing were still going on.

Some of the people she had seen with their eyes closed and seeming to pray were now drinking and carrying on as usual, but there didn't seem to be any fights or any reason for anyone to call the police.

Vicki was half an hour past her curfew, but her parents had never been home this early from a weekend dance before. She expected a loud chewing out, the usual threats of grounding (which were rarely followed through), and charges that she had been involved in all kinds of awful things. All she and her friends had done was to put firecrackers in a few mailboxes and run away, and they tipped over a few garbage cans. Her father always accused her of much worse than that, but his promised punishments were nearly always forgotten.

This night was strange. Her little sister,

Jeanni, was already in bed, but her parents were as awake as she had ever seen them. Her mother sat at the tiny kitchen table, her dusty old Bible in front of her. Vicki's father was excited, beaming, smiling, pacing. "I want to quit smoking and drinking, Dawn," he said, as Vicki came in. "I want to clean up my whole act."

"Now, Tom," Vicki's mother cautioned, "nobody says you can't be a Christian if you smoke and drink. Let's find a good church and start living for God and let him do the work in our lives."

Vicki shook her head and started for her bedroom, but her father called her back. "I became a Christian tonight, honey," he said, a name he hadn't called her since she was a preschooler.

"What were you before?" Vicki asked.

"I was a nothing," he said. "Your mom was a Christian, but I—"

"I knew the Lord," Vicki's mother said, "but I haven't lived for him for years. I was pretty much a nothing myself. But I came back to the Lord tonight. We're going to start going to church and—"

"Church?" Vicki said. "*I'm* not going!"

"Of course you are," her dad said. "When you get saved, you'll *want* to go to church. I can't wait."

"I can," Vicki said. "And when I get saved from what?"

"Saved from hell, saved from your sin. You'll be safe in the arms of Jesus, and you'll go to heaven when you die."

"You really believe that?" Vicki said.

"You bet I do," Mr. Byrne said.

"I'll tell you what I bet," Vicki said. "I bet you'll be drinking and cussing and fighting and losing your job again."

Her father's smile froze. She knew she had made him mad, and she could tell he wanted to hit her. She had spoken what she believed was the truth, but she hadn't really wanted to hurt him.

He approached and reached for her, and she flinched. "Don't you touch me!" she screamed.

He took her gently by the shoulders and spoke softly. "I'm not going to hit you, Vicki," he said. "Let me hug you." She couldn't remember how long it had been since he had done that. "I know this all has to sound strange to you, but something happened to me tonight. It was as if God spoke to me. I don't know why I listened or how he got through, but he did. And things are going to change around here."

That'll be the day, Vicki thought.

"I know you have no reason to believe me,

hon," her dad said. "I don't blame you for not understanding. I've never given you any reason to trust me, so I guess I'll just have to prove it."

"Let's let God work on her," her mom said. "We have enough work to do on ourselves, and he's going to help us with that too."

Vicki finally pulled away from her dad. "Well, I'm glad if this works for you two," she said, "but don't expect me to be part of it. It sounds weird. You hear a crazy preacher for five minutes and now all of a sudden you're holy?"

"We're not holy," her mother said. "We're just giving ourselves to God."

"And you don't think that sounds strange?"

"When God gets through to you," her dad said, "you won't think it sounds so strange."

Vicki finally made it to the little bedroom she shared with Jeanni and flopped into bed. She was scared about what was happening with her parents. She decided that if this really kept her dad from drinking and fighting and being a lazy worker, it would be all right. But this much of a change in such a short time was too much to handle.

Jeanni stirred. "Is that you, Vick?"

"It's me."

"Did you hear what happened tonight?"

"I heard. Go back to sleep."

"Then you know I'm a Christian now?"

"You too?"

"Yup. I got Jesus in my heart."

Vicki sat up. Now her parents were brainwashing her little sister! "Jesus in your heart? What does that mean?"

"Well," she said, "he's not really inside me, but I took him into my life. I'm going to go to heaven someday."

"Oh, brother!"

"You'd better do it too, Vicki. You don't want to go to hell."

"You'd better get one thing straight, Jeanni. Everybody in this trailer park is going to hell, and that includes you and me."

Vicki regretted it as soon as she'd said it. Who was she to be dumping on her little sister? Maybe church would be good for Jeanni, too, as long as they didn't make Vicki go. Jeanni's response proved she had not been bothered by what Vicki said.

"Not me," she said brightly. "I'm going to heaven with Jesus!"

Good for you, Vicki thought. *Just leave me out of it.*

THREE

Lionel— The Liar

LIONEL Washington's parents had moved him out of the inner city of Chicago when he was six years old. His mother, Lucinda, had been a reporter for the Chicago office of *Global Weekly* magazine. When she was promoted to bureau chief, the family could afford to move to the suburbs. They were among the first blacks to live in their Mount Prospect neighborhood.

Now, seven years later, thirteen-year-old Lionel was having trouble deciding where he fit. When he visited his relatives in Chicago, or when his other relatives visited him from the South, his cousins criticized him for "losing your blackness. It's like you're white now."

It was nice to live in a neighborhood where he didn't have to be afraid to ride his

bike anywhere or run with his friends, even
after dark. And Lionel enjoyed having more
things than he was used to having when he
was smaller. His cousins, probably to cover
their jealousy of his nicer clothes and shoes
and the fact that his parents had two cars,
called him "rich boy" and "whitey" and said
he might as well not even be black.

Lucinda Washington was a no-nonsense
woman. She had become a well-paid execu-
tive with the leading newsmagazine in the
country, despite her being black and a
woman. She laughed when her nieces and
nephews teased Lionel. "He's as black as you
are and always will be," she said. "Now you
just go on and leave him alone."

Still, Lionel didn't like it. No way did he
want to give up what he thought was a better
and safer life than he had known. But neither
did he want to be different from his relatives.
There were few other black kids in his junior
high, and none of them went to his church.
His older sister, Clarice, went to Prospect
High School, and his younger brother and
sister, Ronnie and Talia, were still in elementary school.

That made him feel all the more alone at
his school. He grew quieter there and at
home, and he could tell his mother was worried about him. Lionel didn't like the

changes in his body and his mind as he became a teenager. It was too strange. He found himself thinking more. He thought about everything.

Mostly, he thought about his Uncle André. André was the bad apple of the family. He was a drunk and had been known to use and abuse drugs. He'd been in and out of jail for years and once even served a short term at Stateville Penitentiary in Joliet, Illinois.

The thing about Uncle André was that he was a charming guy. When he was sober and out of trouble and working, everybody loved him. He was fun and funny and great to be around. When he was "sick," which was the family term for when he was doing drugs or drinking or running with the wrong crowd, they all worried about him and prayed for him and tried to get him to come back to church.

Uncle André was a great storyteller. He loved to regale the family with exaggerated tales that made them all laugh. He told the stories in a high-pitched whine, making up new things as he went along, and each story grew funnier each time he told it. He would throw his head back and grab his belly and laugh until he could barely catch his breath. Tears would stream down his face until everyone else laughed right along.

That was puzzling to Lionel. How could Uncle André be everyone's favorite half the time and everyone's worry the other half? Lionel's mother told him it was all about understanding and forgiveness. "I don't excuse what he does when he's weak and goes back to doing things he knows he shouldn't," she said, "but when he comes back to church and asks forgiveness and tries to live for the Lord, well, we have to accept him and help him if we can. I believe he's really trying."

Lionel was proud of his mother, but for reasons other than that she seemed wise in the areas of forgiveness and acceptance. The truth was, with her job, she was the star of the family. Not just Lionel's family, but the whole Washington clan. They traced their roots to the freedom riders on the Underground Railroad during the days of slavery, and many of his ancestors had been active in the civil rights movement, fighting for equal opportunities among the races. His mother was one who had proved that a person, regardless of the color of her skin or the housing project she had grown up in, could achieve and make something of herself if she really committed herself to it.

Lucinda Washington told Lionel she had been born and raised in a Cleveland ghetto, but "I loved to study. And that was going to be my way out of the projects." She said she fell in love with journalism, reporting, and writing. She graduated from journalism school and worked her way up finally to *Global Weekly* magazine.

She made good money, even more than her husband, Charles, who was a heavy-equipment operator. He was as proud of her as anyone, and secretly Lionel was proud of her too.

But Lionel had another secret, and it caused him no end of anxiety. Lionel knew something no one else in the family except André even suspected. Neither he nor André were really Christians, even though the whole family history revolved around church.

Church was something that had not changed when Charles and Lucinda Washington had moved to the suburbs. They had been able to somehow fit in to the strange white culture, though many people made it clear they were not happy about a black family's moving in, wealthy or not. The Washingtons had quickly befriended those homeowners who had not moved out and convinced them they were good neighbors.

Finding a church they were comfortable in was another story. Lionel could not remember when he had not been attending church. Family legends said his mother took him to church when he was less than a week old, but his mother told him that was slightly exaggerated. "But you weren't two weeks old," she said, grinning. "You might as well have been born in the church and grown up there."

Actually, he liked church a lot. Lionel was glad that his parents drove all the way back into the city to attend their old church. Some of the people who criticized them for "moving out and moving up" were glad to see they had not forgotten their roots. And even if they were jealous of the Washingtons' ability to move out of a high-crime area, they were glad to see them come back every Sunday morning and evening and every Wednesday night.

Church was what the Washington family was about, but Lionel knew it went deeper than that. His mother not only loved church, she truly loved God. And Jesus. And the Holy Spirit. They had visited a few churches in the suburbs, including a couple that had both white and black members. Lionel had been a young boy then, but even he could see that these just were not the same as his home church in Chicago.

Those people didn't seem to have any

spirit. His mother assured him, "They are certainly true believers, and I don't question their salvation for a second. But I need to go to a church where people don't mind expressing themselves. If I was to jump and shout praises or sing at the top of my lungs, or sway to the music or even dance in the aisles, I wouldn't want to worry about what someone thinks."

Lionel knew what she was talking about. He loved to clap and sing and sway, and while he had not danced in the aisle, he enjoyed watching people who did. The services at his church were long and loud and enthusiastic. People were happy and joyful. He was as happy as anyone when his parents finally realized they would not find their kind of church in their new neighborhood.

So Lionel had the best of both worlds. He lived in a safe place, went to good schools, learned to work and earn and save but also had whatever he really needed, and he got to go back "home" for church twice a week. Every Sunday, his family stayed with relatives between the morning and evening services.

One week while staying with his grandparents, Lionel got to spend a lot of time with Uncle André. Lionel rode along while André picked something up at the store. When André came out, Lionel was surprised to see him followed closely and quickly by two other men about André's age. Obviously not noticing Lionel at first, one of them said to André, "You hear what I'm saying? You get us that money by Friday or you disappear."

André immediately smiled and slapped hands with them, nervously introducing them to "my big sister's little boy." Lionel shook hands with them, but he was scared. He pretended not to have heard, but those guys had clearly just threatened Uncle André. As they drove back to the neighborhood, Lionel asked him about it.

"Them?" André said. "Oh, they're just friends. They were havin' fun with me."

"It didn't sound like it," Lionel said. "I don't like them. They scare me."

André pulled to the curb, several blocks from his parents' home. He took a deep breath and told Lionel, "You're right. They're bad guys. I borrowed some money from them for a deal that went bad, and I don't know how I'm ever gonna pay them back. I'll figure out somethin', or I'll just have to hide out for a while."

"Aren't you scared?" Lionel said.

"'Course I am. But that's my life, Lionel. That's why it's good you're a Christian and bein' raised by my sister. She'll keep you on the straight and narrow path."

"Uh-huh," Lionel said.

"What's that mean?" Uncle André said. "You in trouble already?"

"No, but I was just wondering. I mean, you're a Christian too, aren't you?"

Uncle André looked surprised. "Me? Do I seem like a Christian to you?"

"When you're not, um, I mean—"

"When I'm not gettin' in trouble, you mean?"

"Yeah."

André chuckled, but he looked sad. "You've seen me come back to the Lord lots of times, huh?"

Lionel nodded.

"I'm gonna tell you the truth about that, Nephew, but you can't be tellin' anyone, you hear?"

Lionel nodded again.

"I mean, I don't even want you tellin' your mama. Now listen, those people care about me, I know they do. And I need a place to crash and people to help me get back on my feet now and then. And when I get myself cleaned up and try to start over, I'm serious about it. But the truth is, I tell 'em whatever they want to hear so they'll take me back. If they knew I was serious about surviving but not serious about God, I'd have nobody."

Lionel sat stunned. "So, you're not really a Christian then?"

André sighed as if he hated to admit it. "No, I'm not. Truth is, I don't believe God would forgive somebody like me. I just keep messing up. And every time I go straight, I know I'm gonna mess up again."

"But doesn't God forgive you every time?"

"I don't ever feel forgiven. My family forgives me, but that's because they believe I'm either tryin' or I'm sick."

"But my mom says that's how God forgives people. He uses the people who love them to show them his forgiveness."

"Well, I can't deny my family has done that. But the truth is, I've never been a true believer, a real Christian, and I really believe it's too late for me."

Lionel sat shaking his head. This was sad, but it was also scary.

"So, Lionel, tell me I'm wrong."

"That's the trouble," Lionel said. "I don't know, because I think I agree with you."

"That's not what I wanted to hear," André said. "I was kind of hopin' you were still young enough to believe."

"Well, Mama says you're never too young or too old, and you're never too good or too bad to become a Christian."

"I know she does. Remember, I grew up

with her. But what'd you mean by sayin' you agree with me?"

Lionel wasn't sure how to say it without coming right out with it. "I've never really become a Christian either."

André squinted at him and smiled. "So we're the two secret heathens in the Washington family?"

Lionel did not find it funny. "It's a secret all right. Everybody thinks you're a Christian who has bad spells once in a while. They think I might become a preacher or a missionary someday."

André pulled away from the curb. "You ought to talk with your mother about this," he said. "I'd rather see you grow up like her than like me."

"I can't talk to her," Lionel said. "It'd kill her. She thinks I'm one of the best young Christians she knows. You won't say anything to her, will you?"

"Not if you don't want me to. You could spill the beans about me too, so we'll just keep each other's secrets, OK?"

Lionel nodded, but he didn't feel good about it. He wondered if André was as worried about Lionel's not being a Christian as Lionel was about Andre. "Aren't you afraid it might all be true?" Lionel said. "And that we might end up in hell?"

André parked in the alley behind his parents' home. He threw back his head and cackled that crazy laugh of his. "Now that," he said, "I do not believe. I may have once, but I've outgrown that. Some of these stories and legends about what's goin' to happen at the end of the world, I don't know where the preachers get them. I can't imagine they're in the Bible."

"My mom says they are."

"Well, maybe someday she can show me, and then I'll think about it. Meantime, I'm not goin' to worry about fairy tales, and you shouldn't either."

But Lionel did worry. When they got back to the rest of the family, everyone was gathered around the piano and singing old hymns. Lionel liked that. He sang well and enjoyed blending harmonies. Uncle André sang right along with the rest of them, but once he winked at Lionel. Then he worked his way near him and whispered, "This stuff makes for good singing, but remember, half of it's a good way to live and the other is just fairy tales."

Lionel wondered if Uncle André really believed that. He was a cool guy and older and seemed wise in the ways of the world. If anybody should worry about what happened to him when he died or when the end of the

world came, it should be André. But he
didn't seem worried. He had a plan, a
scheme. He had convinced himself he could
play the game well enough to keep his loving
family around him.

Lionel would rather have been like his
mother than like his uncle, but he knew he
and André were pretty much the same. André
did a lot worse things, but if what Lionel's
mother and the rest of the family believed
was true, Lionel knew that he and André
were the in same boat.

André began dancing to the music, and his
relatives clapped and urged him on. Lionel
couldn't help but smile, seeing his joyous
uncle entertaining everyone. Lionel's mother
put her arm around him as she watched
André. She pulled Lionel to herself and said,
"Isn't the Lord wonderful? Don't we have a
good God?"

Lionel tried to ignore her, but she noticed.
"Hm?" she said. "Aren't you glad to serve a
God who loves you so much?"

"Um-hm," Lionel lied. "Sure, Mama.
'Course I am."

He felt terrible. Like a hypocrite. Like the
liar he was.

FOUR

Ryan— The Skeptic

"YOUR real name's Rayford?" Ryan Daley squealed at his best friend. "We've know each other how long, and I never knew that!"

Raymie Steele smiled and shook his head. "Don't make such a big deal about it. Otherwise I'll tell everybody your middle name!"

The boys had grown up on the same street, one living on each end. They had begun kindergarten together, and now they were both twelve and in the sixth grade. They were as close as brothers. Ryan was an only child, and Raymie may as well have been. His only sister, Chloe, was eight years older and had been away at college two years already.

Ryan and Raymie had a lot in common. Each had a father who was too busy for him. These guys needed each other. Ryan was a little shorter and thicker than Raymie, who was slender and tall and dark like his father. Ryan was a blond and the better athlete of the two.

Like any close friends, they squabbled a lot. Once in a while they even said nasty things to each other and vowed never to talk to each other again. The next day one would call the other or just go to his house, and they would start in where they had left off, best friends. No apologies, no mention of the argument. Just friends again.

They had always gotten a kick out of how close their first names were. That was what had started the discussion of their real full names. Ryan said he had been named after three famous Chicagoans. "My first name comes from Dan Ryan. I don't even know who he was, but there's an expressway named after him. And my middle name, promise you'll never tell a soul, comes from some old mayor from way back when who got assassinated."

"What's his name?"

"I don't want to tell you. I don't trust you."

"If you can't trust *me*—"

"OK, I trust you. But you gotta promise."

"I promise."

"And you've got to tell me a secret you don't want anybody to know."

"I will."

"All right," Ryan said. "The mayor's name was Anton Cermak."

Raymie Steele had doubled over laughing. Ryan couldn't resist laughing too. "So," Raymie said when he caught his breath, "is your middle name Anton or Cermak?"

"Cermak," Ryan mumbled.

"No!"

"Yes! Isn't that awful? And my last name's the same as a former Chicago mayor too."

"I know. How'd your middle-name guy get assassinated?"

"My mom made me look it up. For some reason he was in a parade in Florida with President Roosevelt when some guy tried to shoot the president, missed, and hit Cermak."

"Which Roosevelt?"

"I don't know. Was there more than one?"

"'Course," Raymie said. "Teddy and Franklin."

"Probably Teddy, I guess."

"When was this?"

"In the 1930s, I think."

"Then it had to be Franklin."

"Whatever, Raymie. How do you know all that stuff?"

"I don't know. I just like to study, and I remember a lot of it."

"So it's your turn to tell me something you don't want anybody else to know."

"All right, Ryan, as long as we're talking about names, I'm actually a 'junior.'"

"Your name is the same as your dad's?"

"Yup."

"So his name is Raymond? You're actually Raymond Steele?"

"Nope. It's Rayford."

Now it was Ryan's turn to laugh. They swore to each other that they would never tell anyone else. But when they were alone, they started calling each other Rayford and Cermak. It usually made them smile.

One of the reasons their friendship worked so well was that in spite of all their similarities, they also had individual strengths and weaknesses. Raymie was the student, the one who seemed to know everything and was usually right. It drove Ryan crazy that Raymie actually enjoyed school.

Ryan went to school mostly to play. He was the athlete of the two. You name the sport, he enjoyed it and was good at it and played with all his might. He was the fastest runner, the highest jumper, the best hitter and thrower and even the best basketball shot in his class. Raymie said he considered himself a klutz in sports but that he enjoyed watching Ryan and was proud to be his friend.

Ryan liked it when Raymie stayed overnight at his house or he stayed at Raymie's. Secretly, Ryan believed Raymie had the best dad. Raymie's dad was Rayford Steele Sr., an airline pilot. He always called it "driving" the planes, and the planes he drove were the big ones, the 747s.

Ryan had gotten to go into the cockpit of a 747 once when Mr. Steele had taken him and Raymie to O'Hare. They watched the planes take off and land, and Captain Steele gave them pilot caps, wing pins, and even old computer printouts of weather conditions and route logs.

Whenever Ryan stayed at Raymie's, he hoped Captain Steele was home and would tell him airplane stories. Mr. Steele insisted that his job was actually quite routine and boring. "The important thing is that we do it right and do it safely," he said. He had never crashed, which disappointed Ryan because he thought there would be a great story behind something like that.

The only thing Ryan didn't like about being at Raymie's house was that Mrs. Steele seemed so religious. She always made them pray before they ate, and she often talked about God and even told Bible stories. Ryan enjoyed some of those, but it made him nervous when Mrs. Steele made Raymie say his prayers before going to sleep. Church and prayer and Bible stories had never been part of Ryan's life.

His father was nothing quite as dramatic as an airline pilot. Ryan's dad was a sales manager for a big plumbing fixture company. Ryan was proud that his dad was successful and seemed to make good money. His dad seemed a little upset that, as he said, "I probably don't make as much as your friend's dad, the pilot, but I'm not far behind."

Ryan's mother also worked, so he often came home alone after school. He wasn't supposed to have anyone in the house when his parents weren't there, but for many years he and Raymie cheated on that. They would play and eat and watch television, always keeping an eye out for Mrs. Daley. When she pulled into the driveway, Raymie would hurry to the front door and slip out as she came in the back. Once she was in the house, he knew it was safe to ring the doorbell as if he had just gotten there.

That kept Ryan out of trouble. But one day, a few months before, that had all changed. For a few days, Raymie had excuses for why he couldn't come over after school.

Finally Ryan asked him right out. "What's the deal, Raymie?"

"Well, you're not supposed to have anybody over without one of your parents there, right?"

"Hello!" Ryan said. "We've been breaking that rule for a long time. My mom has never even suspected."

"That still doesn't make it right."

"We'll never get caught, Raymie!"

"I'm not talking about getting caught. I'm talking about whether it's right."

"So, if she catches us, we'll tell her it was the first and only time."

Raymie had shaken his head and Ryan was frustrated. "So you'd make it worse by lying," Raymie said.

"Who cares?"

"I do!" Raymie said.

"Why all of a sudden?"

"I need to talk to you about that."

"Then come on over and we'll talk about it."

"Ryan, you just don't get it. I'm not going to your house anymore when your mom isn't there, OK? You don't have to agree, but that's how it's going to be."

"You're right. I don't get it. What's got into you?"

"Why don't you come to my house and I'll

tell you? Didn't your mom say that if you weren't home when she got home, the only other place you were allowed to be was my house?"

Ryan agreed. A few minutes later they were talking in Raymie's garage. Both Raymie's parents happened to be home. Raymie started right in.

"We started going to a new church, and we've been learning a lot of new things."

"Oh no, not this again! Are we gonna wind up prayin'?"

"No," Raymie said. "This is different. Really. At our old church we believed in God and the Bible and everything—"

"Don't I know it!"

"Yeah, but we were getting kind of bored, especially my mom."

"Your Mom? I thought she liked all that stuff."

"She did, but she said something was missing. Somebody invited her to this new church, and we started going, and we learned a lot more."

"Like what?"

"You really want to know?"

"No, but something tells me you're going to tell me anyway, so let's get it over with."

Ryan had hoped that would insult Raymie just a little and they could get on to playing, but Raymie plunged ahead. "At this new church, New Hope right here in town, they have this really nice old pastor—"

"Wait, the church is called what?"

"New Hope Village Church."

"Weird name for a church."

"Anyway, Pastor Billings is a really nice old guy, but he doesn't just read out of the Bible and then talk about stuff in general like the guy at our other church. Pastor Billings has everybody look up the verses and follow along with him, and he tells us we should read the Bible every day at home, too."

"Every day? Yuck!"

"No, it's great. It's like we can check up on him and make sure we understand and agree and all that."

"But all that boring religious stuff!"

"That's what I used to think too, Ryan. I liked the stories in Sunday school, but when I had to sit in the service, I hated it. I thought I would hate it here, too, but I don't. Pastor Billings says there's more to being a Christian than just going to church and trying to be good. You want to know what he says?"

"No, but keep going. You're gonna be a preacher yourself someday!"

"He says we can know God."

"Oh, come on!"

"No! That's what he says. He showed us

from the Bible that God loves everyone and wants them to know him. That's the reason Jesus came to earth. He was actually God and—"

"Yeah, and he taught us how to live and everything, I know."

"No, 's more than that. He wants people to become true Christians by following him, not just doing what he said but letting him live in our lives."

"Now you've lost me."

"I wish I could explain it like he does. You have to come with me sometime."

"I don't think so."

"Come on! If you told me something was great and important, I'd at least listen."

"Good for you. You think I'm going to follow Jesus or let him, what did you say, live in . . . ?

"Live in your life."

"Too strange."

"I'm just not explaining it right. My mom knows. Let's ask her."

"No! I've heard enough, OK? You know God now, is that it?"

"Well, yeah . . ."

"And that makes you want to follow all the rules and do everything right. Why? So you can get to heaven?"

"No! That's what I used to think. When I'd

do something I knew was wrong—like breaking your mom's rules and everything—I felt bad because I thought that might be enough to send me to hell. I thought if I did enough right things to make up for the wrong things, maybe I'd make it to heaven. But I never knew for sure."

"Now I'm really not getting it."

"That's why you should talk to my mom. We've both received Christ and—"

"*Received* Christ? You're not gonna be like those people that go around knocking on everybody's door, are you?"

"Sometimes I'd like to, Ryan. I want everybody to know."

"So, if doing everything right is not how you get to heaven, why did you all of a sudden become so perfect?"

"I didn't. I want to do right things because I know that's what God wants. But I'm just doing that to thank him for forgiving me and saving me and promising me heaven someday. Know what I mean?"

"No!"

"And you don't want to talk to my mom?"

"No, thanks. What about your dad?"

"Well, we're praying for him."

"So he doesn't go for all this stuff?"

Raymie looked embarrassed. "Not really."

"Well, maybe somebody in this family still has a brain. What about your big sister?"

"We're praying for Chloe too."

"So I'm not the only person you know who thinks this is a lot of baloney."

"That's what you think?"

"Not really, Raymie. It just sounds weird, that's all. And I don't think you even understand it much."

Raymie shrugged. "That's true, but I understand enough."

"Are we done now?"

"I guess."

"Can we play with that model of your dad's plane?"

"I'll get it."

When Raymie left the garage and trotted up the stairs to his room, he left the door that led into the house open. Suddenly Ryan found himself listening in on a strange conversation. Mr. and Mrs. Steele were talking about something even weirder than Raymie had. "Can you imagine, Rafe?" she was saying, "Jesus coming back to get us before we die?"

Ryan heard the rattle of a newspaper. Mr. Steele said, "Yeah, boy, that would kill me."

Now Mrs. Steele sounded mad. "If I didn't know what would happen to me," she said, "I wouldn't be so glib about it."

"I *do* know what would happen to me,"
Mr. Steele said. "I'd be dead and gone. But
you, of course, would fly right up to heaven."

That seemed to shut her up. Ryan heard
Mr. Steele rise. "Come on, Irene," he said.
"Tell me thousands of people wouldn't just
keel over if they saw Jesus coming back for
all the good people."

Now she was crying. "I've told you and
told you. Saved people aren't good people,
they're—"

"Just forgiven, yeah, I know."

Ryan heard Raymie bounding back down
the stairs, just as Mr. Steele was saying, "If it
makes you feel any better, I'm happy for you
that you can be so sure."

Raymie's mother answered softly. "I only
believe what the Bible says."

These people were crazy, Ryan decided. He
wanted to ask Raymie what his parents
meant, talking about Jesus coming back for
people before they died. But he just wanted
to play and think about something else.

He thought that maybe someday he *would*
go along with Raymie to that new church
and see what all the excitement was about.

But he never did.

2

THE LULL

FIVE

The Eve of Destruction

THE evening before the event that would change the lives of Judd Thompson, Vicki Byrne, Lionel Washington, and Ryan Daley, they didn't know each other. Oh, Judd Thompson had seen Vicki Byrne at New Hope Village Church on those few occasions when she was dragged there, all but kicking and screaming, by her parents. But he couldn't have told you her name.

He knew she went to his school, Prospect High. But she was trailer trash. They would not have been seen together. He didn't know, any better than Lionel Washington did, that Lionel's sister Clarice shared a seat on the school bus with Vicki. Judd and Clarice didn't run in the same circles either.

It didn't register with Judd, even when the pilot's name was announced on the 747 flight to London, that the captain also occasionally attended New Hope Village Church. Judd had seen Raymie Steele at church. Raymie was part of the middle school youth group. But Judd didn't know Raymie's name. And he certainly had no knowledge of Raymie's best friend, Ryan Daley.

In truth, the four kids were entwined in a web of connections they knew nothing about. Only the events of that night, mainly *the* event late in the evening, Chicago time, would push them together, a strange mix of most different people and personalities.

Judd Thompson Jr. took a bigger gulp of the champagne than he should have and had to cover his mouth to keep from spitting it out. Some of it came out through his nose, which burned as he coughed. He looked around sheepishly and was relieved to notice that no one had paid any attention. *Ick!* He would just pretend to sip from the glass until the beautiful flight attendant took it away.

Judd had his eye on the two seats ahead of the men across the aisle from him. A rather large man had squeezed his way past Judd to sit in the window seat next to him, and as

roomy as first class seats were, Judd decided
he would rather sit alone if he had a choice.
He had been told at the counter that he had
bought the last seat on the plane, but those
two seats on the other side were still empty.
He hoped whoever had reserved them had
changed their mind or would miss takeoff for
some reason.

But just as the flight attendants were gath-
ering up glasses and napkins and telling passengers to stow their tray tables, a stooped,
old couple boarded and headed for those
seats. The flight attendants had helped the
other first-class passengers store their belong-
ings, but all were busy as the couple made
their way up the aisle.

The young man sitting in the window seat
across the aisle from Judd was shutting
down his laptop computer when he seemed
to notice the old couple. He turned to the
man on his right, the one who had already
loosened his tie and downed three small
bottles of liquor. "Sir, that elderly gentle-
man could use a little help, I think."

"So?" the man on the aisle said. "What do
I look like, a stewardess?"

"Would you let me by, then, so I can help
him?"

The drinking man cursed and turned in his
seat to let the younger man pass. Judd

watched as the old man took off his sport jacket and felt hat and reached for the overhead bin, which was too high for him. The younger man said, "May I help you with that, sir?"

"Why, thank you, son. You're very kind."

"Not a problem."

"What's your name?"

"Cameron Williams," he told the old man. "Call me Buck."

"Peterson," the old man said, extending his hand. "Call me Harold."

Judd was fascinated. Harold Peterson introduced his wife to Buck, and as they all sat down Mrs. Peterson told Buck her husband was a retired businessman and asked what Buck did for a living.

"I'm a writer," Buck said. "With *Global Weekly.*"

Wow, Judd thought. *A big shot. And not that old.*

After takeoff, dinner, and a movie, Judd tried to relax. Most passengers put away their reading material and curled up with blankets and pillows. Soon the interior lights went off, and when Judd headed toward the tiny bathroom, he noticed only the occasional reading lamp here and there. By the time he was back in his seat, the plane was a dark, quiet, humming chamber. He wished he could sleep, but he couldn't get his mind off his family.

When would they discover he was gone? How would they feel? What would they do? Was it too late to just catch a plane back home, apologize, and beg for mercy? No, he was going to see this through. He was going to prove he could be independent.

But boy, he thought, he was going to be tired. When that plane hit the ground in London, he was going to have to find a place to stay. Nervous energy left him weak and drowsy, but there was no way he could keep his eyes shut. Too much to think about.

For two years since her parents had become Christians in the most bizarre way at that trailer park dance, Vicki Byrne had watched for them to fail. She was embarrassed by what they called "witnessing"—telling other people about Christ. They said they were "sharing their faith" with the people they cared about.

That sounded so much like a cult, like the weirdos who tried to talk to people in airports, that Vicki wanted nothing to do with it. Her little sister was so excited about Sunday school and church that Vicki decided not to hassle Jeanni about it. Her older brother, Eddie, wrote and told her he had begun going to church up in Michigan.

Vicki felt surrounded by idiots. She admitted to herself that she was impressed that her father had quit drinking. He still smoked, but he was trying to quit. He always said he felt bad about that, but she never saw him smoke at church, and he didn't even smoke in the trailer anymore. He often said, "Someday God is going to give me the strength to beat this thing."

Vicki's mother pleaded with her, to the point of tears, to go to church with them once in a while. Vicki finally gave in and asked if they would get off her back if she went to one service a month. They agreed, but she really had gone only three or four times in all. Every time her mother or father reminded her that she was not upholding her end of the bargain, the arguing began. She would swear she had just been to church with them the month before. They would show her on the calendar that she had not. She would yell and scream and walk out. They would plead and cry and pray for her.

When she went to church, she hated it. Sometimes her mother looked at her to see if she had listened to what the pastor had just said, and at other times her mother leaned over and whispered the pastor's last sentence. "Get out of my face!" Vicki hissed at her. Again, her mother fought tears.

Vicki didn't understand herself. Often she asked herself why she had to be so mean, so angry. It was obvious that this . . . this thing, whatever it was, was working. Her dad was a new man. He never missed work, was always on time, got promoted, had more friends. He was always sober. He looked happier. The only sore point in his life, besides his smoking, was Vicki. She could see him getting more and more frustrated with her, and she had to admit her goal was to make him explode in anger. Why? So she wouldn't feel so bad about herself.

She had always hated it when he had blown up at her in the past, but this new obsession with church and God was worse. The one time she pushed her dad past his limit, rather than yell, he broke down. "I think the devil's got hold of your soul and he won't let go!" her father exclaimed.

Vicki laughed in his face. "What?!" she said. "You really believe that, don't you? You think we're living in the dark ages and maybe I'm a witch, is that it?"

"I didn't say that," her father said, moaning.

"Don't you see how crazy you all are? Please, just leave me out of this!"

"We don't want you to go to hell!" her mother pleaded.

"At least I'll be with my friends," Vicki said. She had heard people say before that they wanted to spend eternity where all their friends were. She thought it was a pretty sassy line. Her parents just cried all the more. That didn't reach her. It made her sick. After a year or so they couldn't get her to go to church at all.

The only control Vicki's parents had over her was grounding her. She was not allowed to go anywhere or do anything if she stayed out too late. They didn't know where she was or what she was doing, but they had an idea who she was with, and they didn't approve of her friends.

Vicki considered herself lucky that the last two times she had been out past her curfew, only twenty minutes each time, she had been able to slip into the trailer and tiptoe past her sleeping parents' bedroom undetected.

On this evening, though, the same night Judd Thompson Jr. was making his escape from boredom on a flight to London, Vicki Byrne was going out. Her parents would have a fit, she realized, if they knew what she and her friends were up to. They had scored some

pot and were smoking and riding around
with older kids who had cars.

By the time her friends dropped her off at
the entrance to the trailer park, far enough
from her trailer so the car wouldn't wake
anybody, Vicki was already more than an
hour late. Her mother had told her she
would be waiting up for her in the little living room. Vicki felt wasted, and she didn't
want the lecture, the grounding, the tears, the
prayers.

As she came into view of the trailer, she
noticed the only light on was a small reading
lamp in the living room. If her mother was
dozing there, she would surely awaken if
Vicki tried to sneak past. She knew what she
would do. She would slip in the back door. If
her mother discovered her in her bed, she
would swear she had come home on time
and had even tried to wake her mother.

Vicki crept around back, trying not to
make noise in the gravel. She slowly opened
the little-used door and did her best to keep
it from creaking. She held her breath and
pulled it softly closed behind her. She could
see the light on in the living room. She
undressed in the dark and slipped into the
bedroom she shared with Jeanni.

As Vicki lay on her back in bed, she
allowed herself to breathe again. But some-

thing was strange. Maybe the pot had done something to her mind, or her hearing. Normally she could hear her father snoring from down the hall. And she could always hear Jeanni's deep breathing.

Now she heard nothing. Not a thing.

So much the better, she thought. She felt as tired as she'd ever been and was grateful for the peace and quiet that allowed her to drift into a deep sleep.

Lionel Washington always looked forward to the times when Uncle André would come to Mount Prospect and stay overnight. He might be in town for an Alcoholics Anonymous meeting or one of the other half-dozen or so support groups he belonged to. Other times he might just be in the area "on business," though Lionel's mother often asked him not to share what that business might be.

The night Judd Thompson Jr. sat on the 747, unable to sleep, and Vicki Byrne crept into her bed, unable to stay awake, Lionel Washington grew bleary-eyed in his own home.

Lionel's older sister, Clarice, had helped her mother put the younger kids to bed a few hours before. Then she and Lionel and their mother and father sat in the family room as Uncle André told story after story, making them laugh and cry and laugh some more.

Clarice was the first to beg off. "I've got to get up early tomorrow," she said.

Lionel's mother was next. "We're expecting a story to be filed from our London office tomorrow. I can't be late for work. Lionel, when André finally runs out of steam, which I hope is real soon, you two can sleep on the couch in the basement as usual."

"Thank you, Sis," André said. "I won't keep your man up much longer."

He was referring to Lionel's dad, who loved André and his stories. There he sat in his easy chair, trying to listen, trying not to doze. He looked comfortable, a big old working man in a terry cloth robe three sizes too big. He rubbed the corners of his eyes. "Should have taken these contacts out hours ago," he said.

"I'm gonna let you go to bed, bro-in-law," André told him. "Lionel and me will head downstairs."

"Good idea," Mr. Washington said. "I'll just sit here a few more minutes before going up to bed myself. G'night, boys."

Lionel found himself falling asleep next to his uncle in the basement even though André

71

was still telling some story. Lionel was half listening for his father's footsteps above them, which would let Lionel know he had gone off to bed.

But he couldn't keep his eyes open any longer. He fell asleep listening to his uncle's whispering, whiny laugh and only hoped André wouldn't be insulted when he realized Lionel was asleep.

Ryan Daley had very nearly been allowed to stay at his best friend's house that night. His mother had to take the next morning off so she could pick up Ryan's dad at O'Hare Airport. Ryan was to walk to school with Raymie Steele just before his mother was to leave. Both boys thought it might be a good idea if he just stayed overnight with Raymie.

But Mrs. Steele apologized for not being able to have a guest that night. Ryan's mother told him that Mrs. Steele had said that her husband had a flight and that she preferred they do this some other night. "In fact, she suggested this weekend and asked if it was all right if you went to church with them. I told Mrs. Steele that that would be fine."

"Oh, Mom!"

"It won't be so bad, honey. I went to church a few times when I was a kid, and it didn't hurt me any. Just act nice, and they'll be nice to you."

Ryan dreaded even the thought of that, and he wished he could have stayed at Raymie's that night. But he would see Raymie in the morning, and they would have fun this weekend—even if he did have to go to church.

With his dad away on business, Ryan knew his mother would stay up watching television longer than normal. He let her see him in bed and turn off his light, then waited until he was sure she was settled in downstairs. He shut his door all the way and stayed up reading and listening to music.

Ryan was getting drowsy when he thought he heard something. He lifted one earphone, listening for his mother. If she was coming up to bed, she would be able to see the light streaming under his door. He rolled over and flicked off his light, but he heard no footsteps on the stairs. What he heard was a siren, maybe more than one.

He tiptoed to the window and peered out. On the horizon he saw the pink glow of a fire in the distance. Way to his left was another. Then he heard closer sirens. This was a crazy night for some reason. He wanted to see if there was anything on the news, and he wondered if he could convince his mother the sirens had woken him when he padded downstairs.

Ryan carefully opened the door and went down the carpeted steps. He peeked into the television room, where his mother's movie was ending. She was sound asleep. He waited until the credits had rolled and the commercials came on, hoping there might be some news. But as soon as the last commercial played, the national anthem came on, signaling the end of the broadcast day.

He thought about changing the channel, but he knew that would awaken his mother. When the station signed off the air, the static roused his mother, and Ryan hurried back upstairs before she noticed him. He climbed under the covers in the dark and pretended to be asleep when she peeked in on him, as usual.

He was going to put his headphones back on and try to tune in some radio news. But now he was really tired. The sirens seemed farther away, so he just closed his eyes.

3

THE
MORNING
AFTER

SIX

Judd Returns Home

JUDD was so keyed up, so excited, and yet so
worried about what his parents were going to
do when they discovered he had disappeared, he couldn't imagine having fallen
asleep. Yet he had. He figured out how to
make the seat back recline, and he was soon
staring at the dark ceiling, his eyes beginning
to grow accustomed to the low light. He
folded his arms across his chest and forced
himself to breathe more and more slowly.
He had to relax, needed to get some rest if he
was going to succeed in finding a place to
hide out in London.

Hattie, the flight attendant, glided by every
half hour or so, and Judd realized he was
finally starting to unwind when he quit looking forward to watching her. Eventually, the
slow blinking began, then he turned side-

ways and curled up. Now he had to close his eyes or he would appear to stare at the large man in the window seat next to him.

The man had said not one word the entire flight, but Judd noticed he had bowed his head before eating. That Judd would never do, not even in private, unless he was with his family. That was another reason he needed to be out on his own—so he wouldn't be embarrassed by all their religious rituals. His mother hated when Judd referred to her faith as a religion. She had told him so many times he had memorized it, "Christianity is not a religion, it's a relationship with God through Christ."

Yeah, OK, Judd thought.

Judd had no idea how long he had been sleeping. In fact, he wasn't sure he had slept at all. And if he had slept, was he really awake now? He was disoriented, in the same position he had curled into, how long ago? He felt as if he had been sleeping and had not moved. But his eyes were open.

Something was different. A blanket! The flight attendant must have draped it over him. He looked at his watch. Not quite eleven at night, four in the morning out over the Atlantic. He knew the plane had to be nearly halfway between England and the States now.

The man next to him had a blanket too, but it was folded neatly in his lap. The air flow above him was directed on his face, and Judd imagined him sweating in his sleep. He was spread out over that seat, hands at his sides, head back, mouth open. Judd was grateful the man was not snoring.

With his chin on his shoulder, Judd was just inches from the big man. But that was the way with airplanes. Strangers had to sit close to each other. He looked across the aisle to where the drinker seemed to have collapsed onto his tray table. Beyond him the magazine writer, the one who had introduced himself to the old man, sat sleeping with his back straight, his head down, chin on his chest.

Ahead of those two was the elderly couple, the Petersons. Judd couldn't see the woman. She was small and hidden in her seat. Her husband had tucked a pillow behind him and slept with his head poking out into the aisle. Judd was still barely awake when Hattie came by. She had to avoid the old man as she slipped past. Judd mustered his courage and whispered, "Thanks for the blanket."

She flashed him a smile. "Oh, you're welcome, hon," she said. "My partner, Tony, brought you that. Need anything else?"

He was too tongue-tied to say any more.

He shook his head, turned back to face the big man on his right, and drifted off to sleep again.

Activity behind him nagged Judd to semi-consciousness. How long had he slept this time? It seemed only a few minutes, but it could have been hours. He didn't want to rouse, didn't want to open his eyes. He fought to stay asleep. Someone had said something. Another person was up and about. Someone walked by quickly. Surely it wasn't dawn yet. Sunlight peeking through the window coverings surely would have awakened him.

For a minute Judd heard nothing and was grateful. He brought his watch up to his face and peeked ever so slightly at it. He couldn't make it out. It seemed nearly the same time as the last time he checked. He took a deep breath, then opened his eyes.

The man next to him must have gone to the bathroom. Why hadn't Judd felt him get by? Judd's long legs were stretched under the seat in front of him. No way was that man agile enough to have climbed over him without his knowing. He squinted and stared in the darkness, wondering if he was dreaming.

The flight attended hurried past. No, she more than hurried. She was nearly sprinting up the aisle toward the cockpit. This was no dream. Judd sat straight up and noticed a few others doing the same. He craned his neck and looked back toward the circular stairway that led to coach class. He heard too much activity for the middle of the night. Someone shrieked and another called out, but he couldn't make it out.

Just as Hattie reached the cockpit, Judd saw the door open and one of the pilots mosey out. Hattie nearly bowled him over. Judd couldn't hear them, but it was clear she was upset, maybe scared. Did she know something the pilot didn't? Was something wrong with the plane? Wouldn't that be a kick in the teeth, Judd dying in a plane crash on his first night of freedom! His parents would never understand.

Hattie pulled the pilot out of the aisle and into the cooking compartments. Judd was desperate to know what was going on. He heard a noise up there, as if she had fallen. He leaned into the aisle and saw her on her knees, whimpering. The captain seemed to be trying to comfort her, and she held on to him as if scared to death.

Judd suddenly felt very young and very afraid.

Behind him more people were crying out. What was going on? What were they saying? The young man and the drunk across the aisle were both sound asleep. Judd could no longer see the old man. And the two people in front of Judd must have slid down in their seats too.

The pilot left Hattie in the galley area and stepped out into the aisle, as if studying the seats in first class. Judd pulled off his blanket and tried to catch the captain's eye, to read something on his face. But it was too dark. And the pilot was distracted.

From the seat ahead of him and to the left, he heard the voice of the old woman. "What in the world?" she said. "Harold?"

Was something wrong with the old man? Judd couldn't resist standing to look. Everyone else in first class seemed to be sleeping. He unfastened his seat belt and rose to look at the old couple. The woman sat there with her husband's sweater and dress pants in her hands!

Judd shook his head, trying to clear his mind. What was she doing with her husband's clothes? And where was he? Obviously, that's what she was wondering too.

The pilot hurried past before Judd could think how to phrase a question. All he wanted to know was what was going on, but the pilot and certainly the flight attendant didn't seem to know either. When the pilot reached the stairs, Mrs. Peterson stood and called out to him. "Sir, my husband—"

Judd saw the pilot put a finger to his lips and whisper, "I know. We'll find him. I'll be right back."

And now here came Hattie. Judd said, "Ma'am?" but she didn't answer.

She grabbed the pilot by the shoulders from behind. "Should I turn on the cabin lights?" she asked.

"No," the pilot whispered. "The less people know right now, the better."

What did that mean? Judd watched the two hurry down the stairs. He turned back to see the old woman talking to the writer behind her. He was dragging his fingers through his long blond hair.

"Trouble, ma'am?" Buck said.

"It's my Harold," she said.

"Does he need something?" Buck asked, stretching.

"He's gone!"

"I'm sorry?"

"He's disappeared!"

"Well," Buck said, "I'm sure he slipped off to the washroom while you were sleeping."

"Would you mind checking for me? And take a blanket."

"Ma'am?"

"I'm afraid he's gone off naked. He's a

religious person, and he'll be terribly embarrassed."

Judd still stood, as if glued to the floor in
front of his seat. He watched Buck Williams
climb over the sleeping drunk in the aisle
seat and move up to take a blanket from the
old woman. Buck crouched and studied the
clothes Mr. Peterson had left in his seat.
"Does your husband have epilepsy?"

"No."

"Sleepwalking?"

"No."

"I'll be right back."

Judd didn't want to look down into the
seats in front of him, and he certainly didn't
want to look to his right where the big man
had been. But he forced himself to. Over the
backs of the seats ahead of him he saw blankets, pillows, and full sets of clothes. Glasses,
jewelry, even a man's wig lay on his seat.

His heart racing, Judd looked next to him.
That neatly folded blanket now lay atop flat
trousers that led to empty socks and shoes.
On the back of the seat lay the limp, still-
buttoned white shirt, the still-knotted tie,
and little bits of metal. Judd's knees were
weak. Other passengers woke up and discovered their seatmates missing, their clothes left
behind.

Judd leaned close to the big man's pile of

clothes and turned on the overhead light. He could still smell the man's cologne. And those tiny bits of metal were dental fillings!

Buck Williams moved past Judd's seat. "Excuse me," he said to another passenger. "I'm looking for someone."

"Who isn't?" a woman said.

The pilot rushed back toward the cockpit, followed by his flight attendant. She told Buck, "Sir, I need to ask you to return to your seat and fasten your belt." Hattie turned and gave Judd a look as if she expected the same from him. He sat quickly and refused to look at the clothes his seatmate had left behind.

Buck tried to explain. "I'm looking for—"

"Everybody is looking for someone," Hattie said. "We hope to have some information for you in a few minutes. Now, please."

When Hattie passed him, Judd quickly left his seat and ran to the stairway. Halfway down he saw the cabin lights finally come on. All over the plane people held up clothes and gasped or shrieked that someone was missing. Judd walked stiff-legged back to his seat and heard Buck tell Mrs. Peterson, "Apparently many people are missing." She looked afraid and puzzled.

Judd was afraid too, but he wasn't puzzled. As the pilot came over the intercom, pleading for people to remain calm, the full realization of what had happened hit Judd. He didn't know how many other people on the plane had any idea, but he sure did. Christ had come as he promised and raptured his church. Judd lowered his face into his hands and shuddered. It was the worst nightmare imaginable, and he was wide awake. He, and most of the passengers on that plane, had been left behind.

Judd raised his head when Hattie approached again. Her face was red and puffy, and she breathed fast, seeming to fight for control. She stopped in the aisle, right next to him, and put her hand on his seat back to steady herself. Draped over her arm was a sweater-vest with a shirt and tie still in it. The nameplate dangling in front of Judd read "Tony."

The pilot's voice came over the intercom and announced that cards would be passed out to determine who and how many were missing. Hattie roused the sleeping drunk on the aisle and asked if any in his party were missing. He drooled, his eyes heavy. "Missing? No. And there's nobody in this party but me." He closed his eyes again, and Judd knew he had no idea what had happened.

Later, when the captain announced they were turning around and heading back to Chicago, Judd led the cheering. Home had never sounded so good. His plan—his crazy, stupid, selfish plan—was out the window now. He would pay his dad back for the money he had already taken with the card, and if it wasn't too late, he would get right with God. It seemed strange to even think that way, and he suddenly realized that if he was right about what had happened, he would be going home to an empty house.

Judd dropped his head again and felt the tears come. From across the aisle he heard Buck say to the sleeping drunk, "I'm sorry, friend, but you're going to want to be awake for this."

The drunk said, "If we're not crashin', don't bother me."

In spite of their terror, passengers seemed to settle down for the long flight back to Chicago. Judd refused all offers of food and beverage, unable to think of anything but what he might find at home.

As the heavy plane retraced its route across the Atlantic, it retreated from the rising sun. The pilot announced that they were going all the way back to Chicago because most other airports were jammed and closed. He also said to expect chaos on the ground because these disappearances had happened everywhere around the world at the same time.

Judd saw Hattie and Buck talking. She told

him that even more bizarre than the vanishings was the fact that every single little child
on the plane had disappeared. Many adults
and some teenagers, but *all* the babies. That
awakened the sleeping man on the aisle.
"What in blazes are you two talking about?"
he said.

"We're about to land in Chicago," Hattie
said. "I've got to run."

"*Chicago?*" the man demanded.

"You don't want to know," Buck said.

Judd looked out the window as the plane
cut through the clouds and offered a view of
the Chicago area. Smoke. Fire. Cars off the
road and smashed into each other and trees
and guardrails. Planes in pieces on the
ground. Emergency vehicles, lights flashing,
picking their way around the debris.

As the airport came into view, it was obvious no one was going anywhere soon. There
were planes as far as the eye could see, some
crashed, some burning, the others gridlocked
in line. People trudged through the grass
toward the terminals. Cranes and wreckers
tried to clear a path through the front of the
terminal so traffic could move, but that
would take hours, if not days.

The pilot announced that he would have
to land the plane two miles from the terminal and that passengers would have to slide

down inflatable emergency chutes to get to the ground. All Judd cared about was getting on the ground. He would run all the way to the terminal, where he could call home. He would ask someone how he could get home, and he was willing to pay any amount. He had that credit card and wads of cash in his pocket.

Half an hour later, when Judd came huffing and puffing past the crowds and into bigger crowds in the terminal, he saw lines a hundred long waiting for the phones. On TVs throughout the terminal he watched news stories from around the world of people disappearing right out of their clothes in front of the camera. A nurse vanished as a woman was about to give birth, and the baby disappeared before it was born. A groom disappeared as he was putting his bride's ring on her finger. Pallbearers at a funeral disappeared while carrying a casket, which fell and popped open, revealing that the corpse had vanished too.

Judd raced outside and through the jammed cars, following lines of people to cabs and limousines. He sprinted to the front and stuffed a huge roll of bills into the driver's hand. Judd told him his address, and the man pulled away.

It took two hours to pick their way

through the results of crashes and fires. The limo driver said, "Some people disappeared with stuff cooking on the stove, and there was no one there to turn it off. That's why you see so many homes burned or burning."

When they finally reached Judd's street in Mount Prospect, the driver stopped and said, "There you go, son. Sure hope you find what you're expecting."

"I hope I don't," Judd said.

SEVEN

Vicki's Sad Awakening

DAWN came way too soon for Vicki Byrne. The morning sun poured through the slatted window at the back of the house trailer where she shared a tiny bedroom with her little sister.

Vicki lay on her stomach and felt as if she hadn't moved since shortly after she had collapsed into bed. The buzz from the marijuana was long gone, but she still tasted the stale tobacco from the cigarettes and was hung over from several too many beers. She wondered how soon her mother would come to get her up. Vicki had purposely not set her alarm. Her mother usually roused her just before she left for work and just in time for Vicki to dress, eat, and make the school bus.

That usually happened shortly after Vicki smelled breakfast, or at least coffee coming from the kitchen situated just this side of the living room. This morning she smelled something metallic, but not food. She heard nothing. Was it still too early? Usually after a night like she'd had, her mother would have to shake her to wake her.

She felt as if she could sleep a few more hours. What time was it, anyway? Vicki lifted the covers and rolled to her back. Jeanni was already up. Why couldn't she hear her? Vicki sat up and stretched, rubbing her eyes. Strange. Jeanni's school clothes were still set neatly on her chair. *She must be in the bathroom*, Vicki decided. She lay back down and waited for her mother.

Half an hour later, Vicki awoke quickly and looked at the clock for the first time. What was this? Had her parents given up on her altogether? They both had to be gone to work by now. Had Jeanni gone off to school in her play clothes?

Vicki dragged herself out of bed. She didn't know what it felt like to be an old woman, but it couldn't be much different from this. She was stiff, and her whole body ached. She padded down the hall to the bathroom, realizing she was the only one in the trailer. On her way back to the bedroom she suddenly stopped. Something was wrong. She backed up two steps and looked out the window to the asphalt apron.

Vicki squinted and shook her head. What in the world? Her dad's pickup and her mom's little rattletrap of a car were still there! Occasionally one of them would drive the other to work if one of the vehicles wasn't running. And once in a while one of them might get a ride to work with someone else. But both of them? On the same day? Vicki stood staring out the window, trying to make it compute.

Finally, she was convinced, she had figured it out. She hadn't heard anything because she had slept too deeply. Her sister probably dressed for a field trip. And for some reason, something was wrong with both cars on the same day. No big deal. Her mother had not tried to awaken her because she was mad at her. Mom had probably fallen asleep in the living room waiting for her to get home, knew Vicki was late but somehow missed her sneaking in. Just for that, Mom wouldn't get her up in time for school.

So what? Vicki thought. *I can blame it on Mom for not getting me up, and I can get more sleep.*

Then she smelled it. Something acrid. Something burning. And it was *in* the trailer! She hurried into the kitchen, where the tea-pot was smoking on the stove. The ceramic paint was black, the pot misshapen and clearly dry. Vicki's mother often liked tea late at night, but it wasn't like her to leave the pot on the stove until the water had evaporated away.

Vicki grabbed a pot holder before reaching for the handle, which had nearly melted. Even through the thick cloth the pot was searing hot. She dropped it in the sink, where it hissed in the water. What was water doing in the sink? Her mother never let dishes soak. She drew water only when she was ready to do all the dishes, and she always did them all and emptied the sink.

Vicki turned off the burner and looked around. Her mother had not even gotten out her teacup yet. She had never known Mom to forget water she had put on to boil, and certainly not overnight. What was going on?

Something out the window caught Vicki's eye. It was one of her friends, an older girl, wandering between trailers. Vicki swung open the door. "Shelly! Shelly, what's up?"

But Shelly didn't even turn. She just kept walking, as if in a trance. Still in her pajamas, Vicki stepped outside and yelled at her friend. Still she didn't turn. Vicki darted back in and threw on a top, shorts, and slip-on shoes. She trotted down the road until she was right behind Shelly. "Hey, girl!" she said. "What's the matter with you?"

Shelly turned and faced her, pale and trembling. "Shel, what happened? Are you all right?"

"Haven't you heard?" Shelly said, looking at Vicki as if she were a stranger.

"Heard what? What's going on?"

"People are missing," she said. "Disappeared. Vanished. Right out of their clothes. Watch the news. It's all over the world. Three trailers here burned to the ground. Lots of people lost family. Mrs. Johnson vanished late last night drivin' her husband home from the bus stop. He couldn't grab the wheel in time, and the car hit a tree. He's hurt real bad."

"Shelly, are you high? drunk? walking in your sleep? What?"

Shelly turned and walked away. Vicki called after her, but Shelly didn't respond. Vicki looked down the road to the cluster of trailers at the end of her area. People milled about, talking. Were all these people off work? She stepped off the road as a fire truck left the area. Could Shelly be right?

Vicki hurried back to her trailer and stood on the top step to survey the area. She saw two trailers that were now just charred remains, one with smoke still rising. People held each other, crying. She didn't want to go back inside, afraid of what she might find. But she had to.

She pulled the door closed behind her as she stepped back into the living room. Where was the remote? Her mother didn't like late-night TV. She would have stayed up reading. For the first time, Vicki looked at the chair where her mother would have been waiting for her the night before. Her mother's slippers were on the floor in front of the chair. Curlers and hairpins were strewn about, as if they had been dropped. Her mother's flannel nightie and thin robe were draped over the chair. Her Bible appeared to have fallen, hit the chair, and flipped over, landing page-side down on the floor, forming a little black tent.

What was that in the middle of the chair, atop her nightclothes? Vicki slowly moved closer. It was her mother's dental plate, the metal bridge with a porcelain tooth she was so self-conscious about. She never took it out in front of anybody, thinking it made her look old to have bridgework in her mouth from a childhood bike accident.

Vicki could barely breathe. Hands shaking, her whole body shuddered as she turned on the television. ". . . these grisly scenes from around the world," the announcer was saying, "evidence of the mass disappearances that occurred in every country at approximately midnight, Eastern Standard Time. . . ."

She was light-headed, and her stomach churned. This had to be a dream. She felt her way to a chair, unable to take her eyes from the screen. She pinched her arm and winced. No dream. "Here again," the newsman said, "is one of the strangest images we have received from this phenomenon no one can explain. This video was shot by the uncle of a soccer player at a missionary boarding school in Indonesia. Watch as the players race down the field. In slow motion now, watch as all but one player disappears. Their uniforms float to the ground as the ball bounds away and the sole remaining player stops and stares in horror. Watch as the cameraman keeps the video rolling and turns from side to side, showing he is one of few adults remaining, the rest having also disappeared right out of their clothes."

Vicki heard a throaty moan and realized it was her own. As the TV droned on and bizarre images came from everywhere, she made her way to her parents' bedroom. Her father's leather necklace, the one that so embarrassed her, lay on his pillow. The necklace had the initials W. W. J. D. carved into it, which her father proudly told her reminded him that in every situation he was to ask himself, "What Would Jesus Do?"

An empty drinking glass lay on the bed in a drying circle of water. Dad liked a glass of ice water in bed almost every night. Vicki forced herself to squeeze between the foot of the bed and the wall and moved to her dad's side of the bed. She pulled the covers back to reveal his T-shirt and boxers, the only things he ever wore to bed.

Where were her mom and dad? Where *could* they be? What had happened to everyone? What would she do? Had Jeanni discovered them missing? And if she had, why hadn't she awakened Vicki? *Oh, no!* she thought. *Not Jeanni too!*

Vicki scrambled over her parents' bed and headed down the hall to her and Jeanni's room. A sob rose in her throat, and she felt dizzy. She whipped the covers off Jeanni's bed and saw Jeanni's goofy little kangaroo pajamas.

What was she going to do? Where could she go? She had been so awful to her parents, and now they were gone. Vanished. Would they be back? *Why them and not me?*

And suddenly it hit her. Was it possible? Could it be? Had they been right? Had she been as stubborn and stupid as a person could be? Had she seen the dramatic changes in their lives and still not believed any of the

God stuff? Had they gone to heaven and left her behind?

Vicki moved to the phone and speed dialed her brother in Michigan. "I'm sorry," she heard, "all circuits are busy now. Please try your call again later."

Vicki pulled up a chair and hit the redial button a hundred times in a row, crying but trying to keep from becoming hysterical. How close had she come to being burned up in a fire just like the one that had cost her neighbors their trailers? The TV showed picture after picture of huge chain-reaction car crashes, plane crashes, ships running aground. There were reports of suicides, including the only soccer player who had been left on that field in Indonesia. Others had been killed in accidents caused by drivers disappearing.

Finally, Vicki's call got through. She nearly lost control when her brother's phone rang four times and the answering machine picked up. She waited through the message and then pleaded with him, in tears, to answer. "Eddie, are you there? It's Vicki! Please pick up if you're there! Please be there! Eddie, please!"

Someone came on the line. "Vicki?"

"Eddie?!"

"No, this is Bub." Vicki knew the name but had never met Eddie's roommate.

"Is Eddie there?"

"Uh, no. No, he's not."

"Have you seen what's going on, Bub?"

"Who hasn't, kid?"

"Then you know what I want to know."

"Are you sure, Vicki? I could just as easily tell you I have no idea where he is, just that he's not here."

Vicki sobbed. "But that isn't true, is it? You found his clothes or something, didn't you? He disappeared along with all those other people, didn't he?"

"You'd better let me talk to your mom or dad."

"Bub! They're not here! They're gone, right out of their clothes. My little sister too! Now tell me about Eddie!"

"OK, listen, honey, I didn't see this myself, all right? This is all secondhand, but Eddie was working second shift last night, three in the afternoon to eleven. I was off and we were going to meet at an all-night diner at midnight. I waited for him for about twenty minutes, and I never knew him to be late for a meal. I called the plant, and they said he had left there at about eleven-thirty."

"Wait," Vicki said, "what time is it there now?"

"We're on Eastern Time, sweetie. An hour ahead of you."

"Oh. And please quit calling me little girl names. I'm fourteen!"

"Sorry, Vicki. The picture Eddie showed me must have been when you were little."

"He showed you a picture of me?"

"He bragged on you all the time. So, anyway, a guy comes in the diner who knows us, and he asks me am I waiting for Eddie. I say yeah, and he says Eddie was in a wreck a couple miles up the road. I ask him is Eddie all right, and he says they couldn't find him. All his clothes and stuff were in the car, but he was gone."

Vicki was crying.

"The guy tells the diner guy to get the TV on, that people have disappeared all over the world. The waitress runs to a booth in the back and screams. She says, 'I thought those guys had sneaked out on their bill! Their suits are all still here!' She about fainted. Anyway, we all watched TV for a while, then I came home. You know where all these people are, don't you?"

"I think I *do*, Bub. Do you?"

"Eddie talked about it all the time. He told me about your mom and dad getting religion— 'saved' he called it. He starts going to church, and he gets saved. Dragged me along a couple of times, but it wasn't my thing, you know. You think that could be it? They're all in heaven?"

"I don't know what else to think," Vicki managed. "What else could it be?"

"You gonna be all right?"

"I don't know what I'm going to do."

"You want me to come down there and look after you? Far as I know I didn't lose any family but maybe a couple of other friends."

"Don't worry about me, Bub. I usually ride the school bus with a black girl who knows all about this stuff. I'm going to try to find her. I hope she's still around."

"Good luck," Bub said. "This is really wacky, you know?"

That seemed to Vicki a pretty mild thing to say about the craziest thing that ever could have happened in history. She hung up and turned all the way around. From where she stood she could see her mother's bedclothes in the chair, her father's T-shirt in the bed, and the door to her and Jeanni's bedroom down the hall.

Vicki didn't know what to think. Part of her was glad her family was right. She wouldn't wish her own feelings on anyone, especially on people she loved. Loved. Yes, she realized, she loved them. Each of them.

All of them. She only hoped they *were* in heaven. It wasn't like they were dead.

But they might as well have been. She had become an orphan overnight. And all of a sudden all those so-called friends of hers, the waste-oids who hid from their feelings and their problems behind a buzz of booze and pot, didn't interest her in the least. The girl she wanted to find was the one she often sat with on the bus, the one who had tried to explain to her what had happened to Vicki's parents when they "got saved."

Vicki looked in the phone book under Washington. There were dozens of them, and she didn't know Clarice's father's name. She dialed every Washington whose name began with an *A* or a *B* and about half of them whose names began with a *C*, but none knew a Clarice Washington. Then she remembered that Clarice had said her mother worked at *Global Weekly* magazine.

Vicki looked up that number and dialed. She was told that Mrs. Washington was not in yet and that no, they could not give out her home number. "Is it an emergency, young lady?"

"It sort of is," Vicki said. "I'm a friend of her daughter Clarice, and I need to talk to her."

The woman at the magazine told Vicki she would call the Washington home and pass on her message. "I'm sure she'll call you," the woman said.

EIGHT

Lionel and Uncle André

THERE was no clock in the basement of the Washington home where Lionel and his uncle slept soundly. Lionel never had to worry about getting up on time. His father made some racket before he pulled out at six every morning. Then Lionel's mother made sure everybody was up and in the process of getting ready for school by the time she left at seven. "I don't know what you kids are going to do when you're out on your own," she often said. "I'm creating monsters who don't move till they're told."

It seemed too bright, too late when Lionel awoke. He had always been a slow riser, in a cloud until he got up and moved around, went to the bathroom, got breakfast. This morning he didn't feel like moving. He merely opened his eyes, squinted at the sun rays that had somehow found their way through the tiny basement windows, and watched the dust dance in the columns of light.

Lionel was on his back, staring at the floorboards, wiring, and ductwork in the basement ceiling. This was a scary place in the dark of night. He never slept here alone.

Lionel had a vague recollection of André slipping out of bed, sometime after midnight, he guessed. André sometimes sneaked out of the house for a smoke. Because André always slept so soundly after that, Lionel's father once wondered aloud if André was smoking something stronger than tobacco. And when André spent more time than necessary in the tiny bathroom in the basement, even Lionel wondered if he was taking drugs.

When André came back from whatever he was doing, he would collapse onto the sofa bed with Lionel and wouldn't seem to move a muscle for hours. It was not uncommon for Uncle André to still be sleeping, in the same position, even after Lionel's mother had come down to roust Lionel out of bed. They might argue or crab at each other—usually just in fun—and they were never quiet. But Uncle André would remain dead to the world.

Once, Lionel's mother had made the mistake of trying to rouse André too. He was so out of it and so angry that she just apologized and never tried again. He got up when he got up, and that was often very late in the morning. This morning Lionel couldn't even hear André breathing. He turned to make sure his uncle was alive.

There he lay, on his stomach, his face turned away from Lionel. The slow, rhythmic heaving of his back told Lionel that André was fine. But he sure was quiet.

Lionel heard the phone ring upstairs. His mother or Clarice would answer it. They always did. Lionel's father often urged his wife to let the answering machine screen calls when they were trying to get ready for work and school or when they were having a meal or sleeping. But Lucinda Washington made it clear to the family that she hated answering machines. Theirs was off as long as anyone was in the house. The last one out could turn it on "so it can serve the purpose it was designed for," she would say. "Not so we can screen calls or get lazy. It's for catching calls when we're away, period."

This morning the phone kept ringing, and Lionel heard no footsteps upstairs. Maybe it was earlier than he thought. He sat up, feeling that fogginess and heaviness that made him move so slowly every morning. No one was answering the phone. What time was it, anyway?

Lionel groaned and whipped off the blankets. Uncle André did not stir. Lionel felt the chill of the basement as he moved stiff-legged toward the stairs. Passing a window, he noticed his father's pickup truck in the driveway, blocking the garage door where his mother's car was parked. *It is early*, Lionel decided. *Who'd be calling at this time of the morning?*

Lionel was in his underwear, and his mother didn't want him "parading around that way, now that you're a teenager," but he thought she might forgive him if he answered the phone for her. But why wasn't she or Dad answering it? They had an extension phone on their bed table.

The phone rang and rang, but Lionel was in no hurry. The phone was never for him anyway. He would answer it only because it woke him and there was nothing else to do. Anyway, he was curious.

The kitchen was at the top of the stairs. The lights were off. No one was up. He reached for the phone. It was Verna Zee from his mother's office. "Hi, hon," she said. "Lionel, isn't it?"

"Yes, ma'am."

"Is she there?"

"Who?"

"Your mother, of course."

"Um, I think so. She's not up yet."

"Not up? She's usually the first one here."

Lionel glanced at the wall clock, stunned. It was late morning. "Uh, I'm pretty sure her car's still here. You want me to wake her?"

"No. I work for her, not the other way around. The only reason I let the phone ring for so long is that I know someone's always there if the machine doesn't pick up."

"Um-hm." Lionel wished he were still in bed.

"It's just that on a big news day like this, I'd expect her before now."

"Um-hm." Lionel had no idea what Verna was talking about, and neither did he care. Big news for adults was rarely big news for him. "You want me to tell her you called?"

"Please. Oh, and I also have a message for your sister."

"Which one?"

"Clarice. Her friend Vicki called and wants Clarice to call her. You know her?"

"No, but I've heard 'Reece talk about her."

"Well, she sounds real anxious to talk to Clarice." Verna gave him the number, and Lionel promised to pass along the message.

Lionel didn't want to know why everyone was sleeping in. He just wanted to enjoy it.

He could head back downstairs and catch some more sleep. If the phone didn't wake anyone, why shouldn't he? He glanced at the calendar. It was no holiday. Nothing was planned but work and school. He had started back downstairs when he stopped and turned around.

Wait, he thought. *I could be a hero. I could be the one who keeps everybody from being even more late.*

Lionel went from the kitchen through the dining room toward the stairs that led to the upstairs bedrooms. He opened the door when he noticed something in his peripheral vision. On his dad's easy chair lay the over-sized terry cloth robe. Lionel stopped and turned, staring at it. He had never known his father to take his robe off outside the bed-room. Though he slept in pajamas, he considered it impolite to "walk around in public in them," he always said, referring to his own family as the public.

Maybe he had been warm. André and Lionel had gone to the basement while Dad was still sitting there, nearly dozing. Maybe he shed his robe while half asleep, not thinking. But that wasn't like him. He had always taken great pride in "not being one of those husbands whose wife always has to trail him, picking up after him."

Lionel moved into the living room, where he noticed his father's slippers on the floor in front of the chair. The robe lay there neatly, arms draped on the sides of the chair almost as if Dad's elbows still rested there. When Lionel saw the pajama legs extending from the bottom of the robe and hanging just above the slippers, it was obvious his father had disappeared right out of his pajamas and robe.

Though Lionel was always unhurried and deliberate in the logy mornings, now it was as if life itself had switched to slow motion. He was not aware of his body as he carefully advanced, holding his breath and feeling only the pounding of his heart. The harsh sunlight shone on the robe and picked up sparkling glints of something where Dad's lap should have been.

Lionel knelt and stared at his father's tiny contact lenses, his wristwatch, his wedding ring, dental fillings, his dark brown hearing aid, the one he was so proud of because he had saved until he could afford one that would truly blend with his skin color.

Lionel's hands shook as he forced himself to exhale before he exploded. He felt his lips quiver and was aware of screams he could not let out. He crept forward on his knees and opened the robe to find Dad's pajamas

1 1 1

still buttoned all the way up. Lionel recoiled and sat back, his feet under him. Suddenly it hit him. He lowered his face to between his knees and sobbed. If this was what he feared it was, he knew what was upstairs. Empty beds. Nightclothes.

But would everyone be gone? He didn't want to horrify himself. He didn't want to see everything that had been left behind, just as he was. He just wanted to know whether he was alone. Lionel ran to the stairs and bounded up two at a time. Little Luci's bed was empty. So was Ronnie's.

Lionel was out of breath. He didn't want to panic, but he couldn't control his emotions. It was too perfect that in Clarice's tiny room, her open Bible lay on her pillow. He imagined her there, as he had noticed so many times, lying on her stomach, reading.

The master bedroom was more than he could bear. His parents' bed was still made, his mother's bedclothes draped on one side where it was clear she had been kneeling in prayer. How Lionel wished he had been taken to heaven with his family and that he had been found reading his Bible or praying when Jesus came.

Only for the briefest instant did Lionel wonder if he were dreaming. He knew better. This was real. This was the truth. All doubt

and question had disappeared. His family
had been raptured as his church, his pastor,
and his parents had taught. And he had been
left behind.

He had wanted to believe his Uncle André
when he said that living a good life was one
thing but that all this about pie-in-the-sky
by-and-by and heaven and the Rapture was
just so much mumbo jumbo. Lionel realized
that he believed even more than André did,
but since he had never done anything about
it, he had missed out.

Uncle André! He was still in the basement,
and for all Lionel knew, was still sound
asleep. Tears streaming down his face, Lionel
hurried back down, forcing himself not to
look at his dad's empty clothes on the chair
on his way to the kitchen and the basement
stairs. On the table he noticed the message
he had just written to Clarice from her friend
Vicki. He grabbed it and bounded down the
steps.

Lionel yanked on jeans and a shirt and was
lacing up his sneakers as he called out to
André. "You'd better get up, man," he
whined, feeling the sobs in his throat. "We're
in big trouble."

But André didn't stir. Lionel sat on the
edge of the couch and stared at his uncon-
scious uncle. How he would like to blame

André, anybody, for his own failure. But he couldn't. He knew everything his family knew. He had simply not bought into it. The question now was, was it too late? Was there any hope for someone who had been left behind?

He suddenly felt older and wiser than his uncle. And André didn't seem all that cool and wise anymore. Lionel knew something André didn't, that they had both been wrong, dead wrong. What was the use of waking André now? He would learn the truth soon enough. Let him sleep in ignorance, Lionel decided. This news would ruin the rest of his life.

Lionel trudged back up to the kitchen and slumped into a chair near the phone. Was anyone from his church left behind besides him and André? He called the church, and the answering machine picked up, the pastor's voice announcing when Sunday's and Wednesday's services were scheduled. He concluded, "And remember: Keep looking up, watching and waiting, for the time of the Lord draweth nigh."

Lionel stood to hang up the phone as the announcement continued about leaving a message after the tone, but suddenly someone picked up the phone. "Hello? Hello? Is anyone there?"

"Yes!" Lionel said. "Who's this?"

"This is Freddie."

"Freddie, this is Lionel. Who else is there?"

Freddie was chairman of the trustee board, the committee that took care of the church and also supervised the ushers. Freddie was often at the church, working or organizing the maintenance.

"Nobody, Lionel. Nobody else is here but me. Old Mr. Hazel's clothes are here, but he was the only one in the building last night, playing night watchman when the trumpet sounded."

"When the *what?*"

"Oh, I didn't hear it, Lionel. If I'da heard it, I'd be gone and so would you. But you're calling just like everybody else who's calling this morning. You missed it just like me, didn't you? And you're the only one in your family left, aren't you?"

"I am. Well, except André."

"Is he there?"

"He's still sleeping."

"Get him up and let me talk to him!"

"No, I'm going to let him sleep, Freddie." Lionel didn't dare ask how a man so dedicated to the church could have missed the Rapture.

"I'm coming over there then," Freddie said.

"We, you and I, we both learned a hard lesson today, didn't we, boy?"

"Yes, sir."

"I'm going to talk some sense into that uncle of yours, and we're going to be ready for all the people who come to this little lighthouse looking for answers."

Everybody in Lionel's church referred to it as the little lighthouse at one time or another. "So nobody else from the church got left behind but us three?" Lionel asked.

"Oh, there'll be more," Freddie said. "So far all I've heard from are neighborhood people. I'm praying everybody else who knew the truth acted on it before it was too late, but I imagine there'll be more of us turning up."

"What do we do now, Freddie? Are we going to hell?"

"I don't know for sure, boy, but I aim to find out. And for starters I'm coming to talk to that uncle of yours."

It would be at least an hour before Freddie could get to Mount Prospect, Lionel knew. He wanted to turn on the TV and see what the news said about the disappearances. It must have caused all sorts of chaos. But first he dialed the number Verna Zee had given him for Vicki Byrne.

Lionel heard desperation in her voice. He

identified himself and she immediately said, "Clarice is gone, isn't she? Disappeared."

"Yes."

"And your parents and, what, a couple of younger kids?"

"All gone."

"Oh, God."

"That's what I think too. It was God."

"There's no doubt about that. What are you going to do, Lionel?"

"I don't know. My uncle's here, and a guy's coming from church. I'll be all right. What are you going to do?"

"I'm going to go to my parents' church. I called there, and a guy named Bruce Barnes is waiting for me. He says there's still hope."

"Hope?"

"For us, for everybody left behind."

"Really?"

"That's what he said. He didn't want to talk about it on the phone. But I'm going there. It's not far from your house."

"The white church?"

"I think it's brick."

"No, I mean the white people's church?"

"I guess. I'm going this afternoon. Why don't you come too?"

"I might."

Later, after Freddie arrived and roused André, Lionel answered yet another call.

"Washingtons," he said.

"Cameron Williams of *Global Weekly* calling for Lucinda Washington."

"My mom's not here."

"Is she still at the office? I need a recommendation for where to stay near Waukegan."

"She's nowhere," Lionel said. "I'm the only one left. Mama, Daddy, everybody else is gone. Disappeared."

"Are you sure?"

"Their clothes are here, right where they were sitting. My daddy's contact lenses are still on top of his bathrobe."

"Oh, man! I'm sorry, son."

"That's all right. I know where they are, and I can't even say I'm surprised."

"You know where they are?"

"If you know my mama, you know where she is too. She's in heaven."

The man sounded unconvinced. "Yeah, well, are you all right? Is there someone to look after you?"

"My uncle's here. And a guy from our church. Probably the only one who's still around."

"You're all right then?"

"I'm all right."

From the basement Lionel heard first the laughter from his uncle, who accused Freddie of pulling a practical joke on him. Freddie assured him it was no joke, and André began to cry, then to scream. He raced up the steps, pushing past Lionel. "Tell me it isn't true, Lionel!"

"It's true, Uncle André."

In the living room Andre shrieked at the sight of his brother-in-law's pajamas, robe, and other material items. Lionel poked his head in. "You don't want to go upstairs, André."

But André ignored him and charged up there. Lionel heard loud sobbing, swearing, and doors opened and slammed shut. André barged back down.

"Where's your daddy keep his truck keys?" he demanded.

"Why? Your car is still—"

"My car is trash! Now where are they?" Andre's eyes were wild.

"On the hook next to the refrigerator, but—"

André grabbed the keys, dropped them, scooped them up again, and hurried out. "Aren't you going to get dressed?" Lionel called after him, apparently making Andre remember he didn't even have his wallet.

André ran back in, gathered up his pants and wallet and shoes, and bounded back out in his underwear. He roared away in the truck, and Lionel wondered if he would ever see him again.

Freddie asked if Lionel wanted to go back to the church with him. "No, sir. I'm going to stay here and watch the news. Then I'm going to meet a friend of Clarice's."

"I'll check on you later," Freddie said, and Lionel thanked him.

He made his way slowly into the living room and sat on the couch, watching the horrible news from around the world. Sitting across from his father's empty bedclothes, Lionel had never felt so alone.

NINE

Ryan Left Alone

RYAN Daley awoke early that fateful morning. He had a fading recollection of noise in the middle of the night. It had not been enough to wake him fully, but he remembered thinking his dad had come home. But then he remembered that his dad was not expected until morning. His mother was to pick up his dad after Ryan headed toward the Steeles' to walk to school with Raymie.

Ryan didn't hear his mother and assumed he had risen before her. He took his shower and dressed, then finished his homework before heading down to breakfast. Surely she would be up by now.

But she wasn't there. A note awaited Ryan. It read: "Honey, please stay here until I call you. I'm going to try to get to O'Hare. I'm not sure I'll get through because of everything that's been happening, so please don't worry. And if the stuff on television bothers you, just turn it off. Dad and I'll be home as soon as I can find him. I couldn't get an answer at the Steeles, so don't go there unless you talk to Mrs. Steele or Raymie first. And don't walk to school alone. There may not even be school today. They should say on the news. I'll call you sometime this morning. Don't go anywhere until you hear from me, please. Love, Mom."

Ryan had no idea what she was talking about, but that didn't keep him from worrying.

He got himself some cereal and turned on the little TV his mom kept on the kitchen counter. None of the stations would come in, so he turned it off. When he finished eating, he decided he would call Raymie. The phones weren't working, but he noticed the message light blinking on the answering machine. He pressed the button. His mother had called at four-thirty in the morning. So that was what he had heard. She had left in the middle of the night. And this call came long after she had written the note and left.

"Ryan," his mother's recorded voice said, "I'm stuck in some unbelievable traffic here, and I don't know if I can get to O'Hare or back home. I'll just keep trying. When you get this message, call me on my car phone.

You know the number. I can't get through to O'Hare by phone either, and the first time I tried to call you all the circuits were busy. So if it doesn't work, keep trying. And remember, don't worry. I'll find Dad and we'll get home as soon as we can."

His mother had sounded worried herself. How could he not worry? Ryan still couldn't bring in any TV stations, so he turned on the radio and hooked up his video games. He was immersed in his favorite game when he realized what was happening. It was like a scary science-fiction movie, the kind he had not been allowed to watch until he turned twelve and which still scared him if he was honest with himself.

Something had happened. Millions of people all over the world had disappeared at the same time. They left everything behind but flesh and bone. Driverless cars, trucks, and buses had crashed, ships ran aground, planes crashed. Wherever someone was in charge of something important and they disappeared, something terrible went wrong.

Ryan yanked his video game controller out of the TV and began searching for any good channel. Finally every channel was suddenly crystal clear, and the newsmen even talked about that. They said that service providers were finding that power, water, and communications were sometimes good, sometimes bad. "If you must make a phone call, be sure it's an emergency and get off quickly to keep lines open as much as possible."

Now Ryan was scared. What if his dad had been on a plane where the pilot disappeared? This had happened just before eleven, when he had first heard the sirens! The news reports told of fires throughout the suburbs and the city of Chicago. In fact, there were fires all over the world where people had put something on the stove, then disappeared and never came back to turn it off. Ryan imagined his mother trying to drive through impossibly blocked neighborhoods. He saw a helicopter view of the expressways, which were like huge parking lots. The only luck some people had was when they were able to get off the highways and try the side streets.

Ryan knew his mother had expected to be home by now and not leave him there alone to see this. He was fascinated by the reports from around the world, and he sat wide-eyed, his mouth hanging open, as video shots showed people disappearing and their clothes floating to the ground.

A tape broadcast from Hawaii showed a birthday party where the birthday girl, her two brothers, and her parents vanished as a neighbor videotaped her blowing out her candles. She leaned close to the cake and took a breath, then she disappeared, and her party hat fell into the candles and erupted into flames. The woman doing the videotaping saw only the flames and quickly doused the fire, then realized that she and another couple were the only people still there. Ryan heard her gasping and trying to talk as she taped the scenes of little piles of clothes all around the room.

When the station replayed the tape in slow motion, Ryan saw what the video camera woman had not seen. Just before the little girl's hat fell into the candles, the girl had disappeared, and her dress dropped out of the picture.

A video from a helicopter on the West Coast showed cops pulling over a motorist. As one patrolman approached the driver's side and the other backed him up at the right rear of the car, the driver and one of his two passengers disappeared, and so did the backup cop! The patrolman assumed the driver and one of his passengers had ducked down in the seat, so he pulled his weapon and warned his partner, who was no longer there.

The cop put both hands on his revolver and skipped to the back of the car to check on his backup and discovered his cap, shirt, badge, trousers, belt, gun, cuffs, ammunition, and shoes right where he had been standing. The patrolman panicked, screaming at the occupants of the car to come out with their hands up while he scampered behind his own patrol car for cover.

As he crouched there, one woman in the backseat of the car came out in hysterics, screaming that the driver and the other passenger had disappeared. The cop made her lie face down on the pavement, and he cuffed her before searching the car. He pulled empty clothes from the seats, then released her from the cuffs and comforted her as they tried to make sense of it.

By the time the cameraman in the chopper realized what had happened, several accidents had occurred on the same stretch of highway. He pulled back and panned wide to see tractor-trailer trucks hung up on guard rails, cars having plunged down ravines, and even the clothes of a utility worker hanging from a ladder that led to the top of a light pole.

Ryan wished his mother was home, but he didn't think he could speak even if someone was there to listen. This couldn't be real! He changed channels and found the same thing on every one. People were urged to stay in their homes as long as they were safe, and to stay tuned for more information. Ryan tried Raymie's phone again and reached only the answering machine. He did not leave a message. Later, if he dared, he would walk down to the Steele home and see what was going on. He wondered if anyone he knew had disappeared.

Ryan tried his mother's car phone. It rang and rang, but no one answered. He didn't get that usual recording about the cell phone customer having driven outside the service area or already being on the phone, so he knew he was getting through. It wasn't like his mother to leave the phone in the car if she wasn't there, and she always left it on when she had it with her. Ryan couldn't figure it out, and now he was really worried.

He found a station that listed all the crashes of planes that had been due into O'Hare that morning. His father had been coming in from Asia, which was all he knew. One of the crashed planes was coming from there, but Ryan didn't know the time or the number or even the airline. He just hoped against hope his father had not been on that plane.

News helicopters showed scenes from above O'Hare where big jets were parked up and down the runways. People walked from the planes as far as two miles to the terminal, and once there, it was nearly impossible for them to get out of the airport. Traffic gridlocked the road that led into and out of the airport. Ryan watched as thousands of stranded passengers walked through the zig-zagged cars and down the overpasses and exits until they found taxis and limousines that would carry them toward their homes, if they could make it through the tangled mess.

Somewhere out there Ryan's mother was either trying to get to O'Hare to learn some news about her husband's flight, or she had already picked him up and was trying to make her way home. From what Ryan could see on the news, he didn't expect her for a long time. He dialed and redialed her cell phone number, but she never answered. He hoped with all his might it was just part of the communications breakdown caused by so many people disappearing.

Ryan grew panicky, unable to reach anyone by phone and not having any idea whether his parents were safe. He hated to think his mother might try to call him while he was gone, but he had to get out of there. He had to get to Raymie's house and see what was going on.

Ryan tried his mother again, then Raymie's line. Still just the machine. He hung up and ran from the house, down the block, and to the edge of Raymie's property. People were outside their homes, talking with neighbors. Many were crying. They watched as he approached the front porch of the Steele home. He didn't want to appear to be up to anything, so he just sat on the front step as if waiting for his friend, until people seemed to forget about him.

Ryan was going to ring the bell when he realized the drapes were open, the door was unlocked, and it stood open about an inch. There was no car in the driveway, but some-one must have been home. He slipped inside to the bitter smell of burnt coffee. He tiptoed into the kitchen and saw the coffeepot in the sink, still hot.

Ryan knew someone was home, but who? He opened the door that led to the garage. Only Mr. Steele's BMW was missing. Mrs. Steele's car was there, and so was the one Raymie's sister drove when she was home. Raymie's four-wheeler was there, of course, and his snowmobile and his bike. So who was here and who wasn't? He checked the hall closet where Raymie's father's trench coat, flight bag, and cap were stored. Captain Steele was supposed to have been on some long trip to England or somewhere.

Ryan tiptoed upstairs to the bedrooms, past a bunch of family photos on the walls.

Raymie's door was shut. Ryan knocked lightly. No answer. He pushed the door open. Raymie's nightclothes were in a neat pile on the bed, and Ryan looked enviously at the picture on the bedside table of Mr. Steele in uniform near his plane.

As Ryan left Raymie's room, he held his breath. He heard something coming from the master bedroom suite. What was it? Someone was home!

From the hall, Ryan could see all the way into the suite. There, lying face down on the bed, his uniform in a pile on the floor beside him, was Raymie's dad. He appeared to be sleeping, except that his shoulders heaved as if he were crying. Ryan didn't dare disturb him. He slipped back down the hall, down the stairs, and headed for home.

Ryan had a sinking feeling as he entered his quiet house. He turned on the TV and saw lists of people who had been on board the flights that crashed on their way to O'Hare. "We repeat," the announcer said, "it has never been our policy to release names of missing or presumed-dead passengers before next of kin can be notified. However, with such massive tragedies and the impossibility of local law enforcement agencies being able to keep up with the grisly business of inform-ing families, we have been asked to make these names public as tastefully as possible. Remember, if someone you know appears on these lists, it means only that they held reservations on these flights and that their whereabouts are currently unknown."

Ryan covered his eyes and peeked through his fingers as the names slowly scrolled by. He recognized one as the father of a friend of his. Another one or two looked familiar, and all he could do was wonder how many friends had lost family members. Then he saw his dad's name, and he burst into tears.

He turned off the TV and shook his head. It couldn't be. He tried to make himself believe that his dad had somehow survived and would be calling him. But that wasn't going to happen, and he knew it. It would be just he and his mom now. Did she know already? There was no message light blinking on the answering machine. Maybe she wanted to tell him in person. Maybe she didn't even know yet!

He dialed her cell phone for what seemed the hundredth time. It rang and rang, and finally someone answered. It was a gruff male voice. "Hello! Who's this?"

"This is Ryan Daley, and I thought I was dialing my mother's cell phone."

"Uh, you are, son, if your mother's full name is, ah, Marjorie Louise Daley."

"Yes!"

"Where are you?"

"Who is this?"

"I'm sorry, son. This is Sergeant Flanigan, Des Plaines police."

"What happened? Is my mom all right?"

"I'm afraid she's not, Ryan. There was a gas-main leak we didn't know about, and it blew while several cars were in an intersection here. Your mother's been taken to Lutheran General in Park Ridge. You know where that is?"

"No, sir."

"Well, it's—jes' a minute, son. . . . Yeah, OK. . . . Listen, Ryan, you have friends or relatives there that can look after you for a while?"

Ryan wanted to blurt that he had just seen his dad's name on a list of air crash victims, but he didn't. "Why?"

"Son, I hate like everything to tell you this over the phone, but your mother didn't make it. The county morgues are full, so one is being set up at Maine East High School in Park Ridge, not far from the hospital. You'll want to get someone to get you over here in a day or two for identification, but don't try to come right away."

Ryan couldn't speak.

Sergeant Flanigan apologized again. "I'm

sorry, son. You're sure you've got someone there to take care of you?"

But Ryan hung up. Was it possible that the people who had believed in Jesus had been taken to heaven, just like Raymie had tried to tell him? He and his parents and Captain Steele had been left behind, but now both his parents were dead. What was he going to do?

Ryan had no idea, but he was going to try one thing. Raymie's church was less than a mile away. Ryan wasn't in a hurry. He just wanted to walk and think and cry. If anyone was left at that church, Ryan might be able to find some help.

TEN

Finding Each Other

"EVERYTHING all right at your place, Judd?" a neighbor called out as Judd Thompson headed around to the back of the house.

"Don't know yet," Judd hollered.

In truth, of course, he did know. He knew exactly what he would find in that house. The buzz of the champagne was long gone, and he felt suddenly foolish with his scraggly goatee, his wallet full of cash, and that top-of-the-line credit card. *Aren't I something?* He asked himself. *Big man. Big criminal. Big shot. Now I'm an orphan.* He felt like a child, despite his sixteen years.

Judd ran upstairs and checked Marcie's room first. She was the persnickety one, the one who always kept her room just so, dolls lined up in a row, her schoolbooks and the next day's clothes laid out neatly. Two tiny barrettes lay in the dent in the pillow her dark-haired head had left. Judd pulled back the covers, revealing her nightie.

In Marc's room, was which almost as messy as Judd's own, he found socks and underpants in the bed.

He glanced at his own room before heading down to the master bedroom. His parents had been in there, that was clear. They had gone through his stuff, looking for clues to where he might be. Maybe they had called the library to check on him. Somehow, they had figured it out, but he had left no clues in his bedroom. Fooling them, tricking them, putting one over on them had seemed so cool when he was on his way to O'Hare. Now he felt like an idiot.

Judd had a sinking feeling in the pit of his stomach as he descended the stairs. He wanted his little brother and sister and his parents to be with Jesus, of course. That was what they wanted, what they talked about, what they looked forward to. But he didn't want to be alone, either.

He slipped into his parents' bedroom, where the curtains were closed and it was dark. He didn't turn the light on, letting his eyes grow accustomed to the darkness. Judd shut the door and leaned back against it, feeling weak. He hadn't slept much on the plane, and now he was paying for the nervous energy that had kept him awake.

Judd was stunned to see that his parents' bed was still made. Could it be? Was it possible they had not been taken? No! It couldn't be! He whipped the covers back and saw no bedclothes. He looked around the room, now turning on the light. His mother's robe was draped over a chair. This made no sense. He found his father's robe in the closet and held out a flicker of hope. But what was he hoping? That his little brother and sister had been taken and his parents had not?

He ran to the living room, where the truth quickly became clear. The phone receiver was on the floor. From the positions of his parents' sets of clothes, it was obvious they had changed back into them when they realized they might have to drive somewhere to look for him. His dad's jeans and pullover shirt and shoes were in a pile near the phone. His mother's casual outfit lay in a chair where she had been sitting.

Judd returned the phone to its cradle and scooped up the clothes. He sat with them in his lap and smelled the faint scent of his dad's cologne and his mother's perfume. And he cried. They loved him so much, cared for him, worried about him. And look how he had treated them. He held their clothes close to his chest and closed his eyes, realizing he had gotten just what he deserved.

His mother had told him and told him that Jesus was coming again and that it could happen in Judd's lifetime. He knew that was what his church taught, but it had seemed so preposterous. Well, not any more. It had happened, and he had been left behind. What was he going to do?

Judd knew there would be no sleeping, tired as he was. He had to think about how he was going to get the car back from O'Hare. When would that be possible?

What he should do, he knew, was go to his church. His church. He hadn't called New Hope Village Church his own church since he was in elementary school. Who would be left there? Was he the only member who didn't go to heaven? He felt alone in the world, not just in this house. He decided to call the church, just to see if anyone else was around.

The voice on the New Hope answering machine was the visitation pastor's, a man named Bruce Barnes, who had been there for several years. It was clear from the message that he had been left behind too!

"You have reached New Hope Village Church. We are planning a weekly Bible study, but for the time being we will meet just once each Sunday at 10 A.M. While our entire staff, except me, and most of our congregation are gone, the few of us left are maintaining the building and distributing a videotape our senior pastor prepared for a time such as this. You may come by the church office anytime to pick up a free copy, and we look forward to seeing you Sunday morning."

Judd didn't want to wait. He looked for his mother's keys and backed her car out of the garage, only to go a couple of blocks and find all the roads blocked. He returned to get his little brother's bike. He was way past feeling self-conscious. He was on his way to church, and for the first time in as far back as he could remember, he really wanted to get there.

When Ryan Daley came within view of New Hope Village Church, he didn't know what to think. He had been in a church a couple of times in his twelve years, but not this one. A big, dark-haired kid on a small bike came pedaling past him. They looked at each other but didn't speak. Ryan had never seen him before.

The big kid let his bike fall near the front door and hurried in. Ryan was in no hurry. He didn't know who or what he was looking for. By the time he got into the building, the kid who had been on the bike was talking to a man in his thirties with curly hair and wire-rimmed glasses.

"Can I help you, son?" the man asked, seeing Ryan over Judd's shoulder.

Ryan couldn't get the words out. How were you supposed to ask if it was true, if Jesus had taken his people to heaven?

"Did you lose some family?" the man said.

Ryan nodded. "They died," he managed.

"No, they are in heaven with Jesus."

"They didn't get taken," Ryan insisted. "My dad died in a plane crash and my mom in a car accident."

Bruce approached and reached for Ryan. The boy felt self-conscious, but he let the man hug him. "My name is Bruce Barnes," he said. "I'm the only person left from the staff of this church, and I know exactly what happened. I'm going to teach a small group of young people here soon, and you're welcome to stay."

"You're going to teach?"

Bruce nodded. "I know what happened because I missed it. I have a tape from the senior pastor that will help explain. Is that something you'd be interested in?"

Ryan nodded. So did the big kid, whom Bruce introduced as someone from the church family named Judd Thompson. They shook hands. Ryan didn't know any other kids as old as Judd, except for a few cousins in California.

Bruce said he was expecting two more kids to show up. "I got a call from a girl named Vicki Byrne. I invited her, and she called back later to say she had invited a boy named Lionel Washington. When we're all here, we'll get started. I want to tell you my story."

When Vicki and Lionel arrived, Bruce took the four of them into a small office where he had set up a VCR and a TV. "You're not going to understand everything the pastor says," Bruce said, "but still you'll be astounded that he knows what's going on, even though he's gone. More important, you need to know that I have the same story you do.

"I lost my wife and my young children. They disappeared from their beds, and I knew immediately that I had been living a lie. I had been to Bible college and was a pas-

tor, but I always thought I could get by, living for myself and never making the decision
to receive Christ. Judd, I know you and your
family. I'm surprised to see you here, but I'm
not surprised the rest of your family is gone.
You know what happened, don't you?"

Judd nodded miserably. Bruce asked the
others to share their stories. They cried when
they spoke, and they cried when they listened. They had been thrust together by a
tragedy none of them could have ever
expected.

"I know it's hard for you to grasp right
now," Bruce said, "but I have good news for
you. The question you all must have now is
whether there is any hope for you. You
missed Christ when he came, but you are not
lost forever. We're going to live through
some awful days and years, but the Bible is
clear that there will be a great soul harvest
during this time. People can still become
believers and be assured of heaven when
they die.

"That won't take away your sorrow, your
grief, or your loneliness. I can't even imagine
a day when I won't cry over what I've lost.
But now I don't apologize for telling everybody who comes in here how they can
receive Christ. It's really quite simple. God

made it easy. If you want to hear this, just say so, and I'll walk you through it."

Vicki raised a hand. "Are you saying that if we had done this before, we wouldn't have been left behind?"

Bruce nodded.

"And now we can still get to heaven when we die?"

He nodded again. "Everybody want to hear this?" They all nodded. "First," he said, "we have to see ourselves as God sees us. The Bible says all have sinned, that there is none righteous, no, not one. It also says we can't save ourselves. Lots of people thought they could earn their way to God or to heaven by doing good things, but that's the biggest misunderstanding ever. The Bible says it's not by works we have done, but by his mercy that God saves us. We are saved by grace through Christ, not of ourselves, so we can't brag about our goodness."

"But I didn't do anything good," Vicki said. "I didn't even *try* to get to heaven because I didn't really believe any of this."

"What do you think now?" Bruce said kindly.

"I think I was wrong."

"Me too," Judd said.

"Me three," Lionel said.

Ryan said nothing, but it was clear to

Bruce he was listening. This was all brand-new to him, except for what Raymie had tried to tell him.

"The punishment for sin is death," Bruce continued. "Jesus took our sins and paid the penalty for them by dying so we wouldn't have to. He died in our place because he loves us. When we tell Christ that we know we are sinners and lost and then we receive his gift of salvation, he saves us. A transaction takes place, a deal. We go from darkness to light, from lost to found. We're saved. The Bible says that to those who receive him he gives the power to become sons of God. That's what Jesus is—the Son of God. When we become sons of God, we have what Jesus has: We become part of God's family, we have forgiveness for our sins, and we have eternal life.

"After you watch this video our pastor left behind, I'm going to ask you something I never wanted to ask people before. I want to know if you're ready to receive Christ right now. I'll pray with you and help you talk to God about it. It may seem too fast for you. This may be new to you. I don't want you to make a hasty decision when you're still in shock over what has happened. But neither do I want you to wait too long, to put this off when the world is a more dangerous place than it's ever been. Maybe you missed Christ the first time around because you didn't know any better. But now you know. What could be worse than knowing and then still dying without Christ?"

The four kids sat there, each grieving in his or her own way. Judd had been humbled. Vicki felt a fool. Lionel felt a sadness so deep he didn't know if it would ever go away. Ryan was puzzled. Raymie had told him all this, and Ryan had thought it was stupid. He didn't think so anymore.

As they watched the video of the senior pastor, now in heaven, telling what was going on and how they could come to Christ, each felt a sudden closeness to the other. Bruce told them that if they became believers, they would be brothers and sisters in Christ. They could become each other's family.

They would discover their connections later. Judd would one day realize that Ryan was the best friend of the son of the pilot of the plane he had been on. Vicki knew Lionel through his sister, but she didn't know that his mother had worked for the same magazine as a man who had been on the plane with Judd.

For now they were simply four kids from the same town who shared a common horror and grief. Bruce seemed to have in mind for them a future as a small group. That sounded good to each, especially in their gnawing loneliness.

When the video ended, each sat stunned that the pastor had known in advance all that was now taking place. Clearly this was truth. Certainly this demanded their attention and a decision. Each sat staring as Bruce posed the question of the ages.

"Are you ready?" he said. "Will you receive Christ?"

ABOUT THE AUTHORS

Jerry B. Jenkins (www.jerryjenkins.com) is the author of more than one hundred books. The former vice president for publishing for the Moody Bible Institute of Chicago, he also served many years as editor of *Moody* magazine. His writing has appeared in a variety of publications, including *Reader's Digest, Parade*, in-flight magazines, and many Christian periodicals. He writes books in four genres: biographies, marriage and family, fiction for children, and fiction for adults.

Jenkins's biographies include books with Hank Aaron, Bill Gaither, Luis Palau, Walter Payton, Orel Hershiser, Nolan Ryan, Brett Butler, and Billy Graham, among many others. The Hershiser, Ryan, and Graham books reached the *New York Times* best-sellers list.

Four of his apocalyptic novels, coauthored with Tim LaHaye, *Left Behind, Tribulation Force, Nicolae*, and *Soul Harvest*, have appeared on the Christian Booksellers Association's best-selling fiction list and the *Publishers Weekly* religion best-sellers list. *Left Behind* was nominated for Novel of the Year by the Evangelical Christian Publishers Association in both 1997 and 1998.

As a marriage and family author and speaker, Jenkins has been a frequent guest on Dr. James Dobson's *Focus on the Family* radio program.

Jerry is also the writer of the nationally syndicated sports story comic strip *Gil Thorp*, distributed to newspapers across the United States by Tribune Media Services.

Jerry and Dianna and their sons live in northeastern Illinois and in Colorado

Speaking engagement bookings are available through speaking@jerryjenkins.com.

Tim LaHaye is a noted author, minister, counselor, and nationally recognized speaker on family life and Bible prophecy. He is the founder and president of Family Life Seminars and the founder of The PreTrib Research Center. Presently Dr. LaHaye speaks at many of the major Bible prophecy conferences in the U.S. and Canada, where his seven current prophecy books are very popular.

Dr. LaHaye is a graduate of Bob Jones University and holds an M.A. and Doctor of Ministry degree from Western Conservative Theological Seminary. For twenty-five years he pastored one of the nation's outstanding churches in San Diego, which grew to three locations. During that time he also founded two accredited Christian high schools, a Christian school system of ten schools, and Christian Heritage College.

Dr. LaHaye has written over forty nonfiction titles, with over ten million copies in print in thirty-two languages. He has written books on a wide variety of subjects, such as family life, temperaments, and Bible prophecy. His current fiction works written with Jerry Jenkins, *Left Behind, Tribulation Force, Nicolae,* and *Soul Harvest,* have all reached number one on the Christian best-seller charts. Other works by Dr. LaHaye are *Spirit-Controlled Temperament; How to Be Happy though Married; Revelation, Illustrated and Made Plain;* and a youth fiction series, *Left Behind: The Kids.*

He is the husband of Beverly LaHaye, founder and chairperson of Concerned Women for America. Together they have four children and nine grandchildren. Snow skiing, waterskiing, motorcycling, golfing, vacationing with family, and jogging are among his leisure activities.

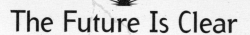

The Future Is Clear

In one shocking moment, millions around the globe disappear. Those left behind face an uncertain future—especially the four kids who now find themselves alone.

Best-selling authors Jerry B. Jenkins and Tim LaHaye present the Rapture and Tribulation through the eyes of four friends—Judd, Vicki, Lionel, and Ryan. As the world falls in around them, they band together to find faith and fight the evil forces that threaten their lives.

#1: The Vanishings Four friends face Earth's last days together.

#2: Second Chance The kids search for the truth.

#3: Through the Flames The kids risk their lives.

#4: Facing the Future The kids prepare for battle.

#5: Nicolae High The Young Trib Force goes back to school.

#6: The Underground The Young Trib Force fights back.